The Many Lives of Nathan James

H.C. Huber

ISBN-13: 978-0997020519
ISBN-10: 0997020512

Edited by Erica Smith.
Cover Design by Meryl Natow.
Cover Photography by H.C. Huber.

Bobeen Publishing
New York, NY

For the mother who encouraged me, the father who guided me, the brother who laughed with me and the husband who believed in me.

CHAPTER ONE
Preface

When the nightmares started, I wasn't afraid. Nightmares are made of fictional monsters and creatures under your bed. Nightmares are for children. But as they reoccurred and took a realistic form, my nightmares turned into memories … memories that rested deep inside the darkest corners of my mind. That was probably the most disturbing part about my dreams. I watched all of these atrocities unfold before my eyes, helpless to put an end to these mistakes … until now.

Dreams are a manifestation of images in your mind strung together by the subconscious to relay a message to the dreamer. These images can be things you see in everyday life but positioned in a new way, or they can be snippets of memories from an entirely different time. This is your mind reaching deep into the storage of your soul's thoughts to fill in the blanks of your life. This collection of images isn't created by your imagination. They have been seen, experienced and stored in your soul for a purpose.

When I began this journey, I had no belief of life after

death. My thoughts on the afterlife were simple: ashes to ashes, dust to dust. The body gives itself back to the earth that nourished it during existence, nothing more. When my father died, I took no solace in a higher entity or he "being in a better place," as I was often told. I believed that my father was simply a small pile of gray dust, spread over the land of his childhood home, save for a small portion left to be buried at a designated site, per his request. This ceremonial spreading of his body was only for the benefit of the living. He doesn't exist in the ash. It was simply a symbolic gesture linking him to a physical place for the sanity of those he left behind. He was just gone. His body was the shell that held him until it became nothing. Ashes to ashes, dust to dust.

This hindered my ability to see my dreams, my nightmares, for what they were – messages sent from the past to stop a vicious cycle. I still don't know if I can believe everything I saw. It was so vivid, like brush stokes in an abstract painting culminating in front of your eyes to create a living scene. I can still smell the gunpowder hanging in the air during the Civil War, feel the weight of a handcrafted sword pulling at my waist as a Viking and see the terrified look in her eyes as she gazed upon the destruction of Pompeii. I have lived over a hundred lifetimes. Lost them over a hundred times, watching them slip though the cracks of my mistakes.

Few people are privileged enough to engage their past selves, which makes it that much harder to believe my story. Quite frankly, there are times it seems unbelievable even to me. But I felt these lifetimes. I experienced the pain. It's carved into my soul like a festering wound. Regardless of my doubts, I chose to believe what I saw. I chose to embrace the nightmares and silence them once and for all. I chose my soulmates.

CHAPTER TWO

Nightmares

The air smells sweet, like a meadow full of honeysuckle after a light rain. Feathery clouds dance gracefully across the skyscape. Bits of pink and gold pierce the blue expanse. The fiery light illuminates the subtle traces of red her hair. We sit wrapped in each other, blissfully silent, watching the sunset paint us a portrait of the evening. I feel fleeting heat clinging to her shoulders and rest my head there, soaking in her warmth. A small chuckle escapes her and I catch a glimmer of a smile. The world stops spinning for a brief moment, just long enough to notice us.

I steal a kiss on the apple of her ice-cold cheek then pull away slightly to look at her pale face. Her eyes are bloodshot and wide. The golden freckle in her left iris stands out.

"Find me, Nate. Don't give up," she whispers. I feel her breathing slow, her eyes now red. Her head falls from my embrace. "Find me." Her arms fall away and her eyes are still.

"Liv! Liv, wake up! Olivia, wake up, please! You're here! You're found!" I bury my head into her shoulder. I feel tears sting my eyes. A raw pain creeps into my throat, but I can't hear myself screaming. I hug her tighter, but her body only becomes more limp. I lift my eyes to meet hers only to watch her body turn to sand. She slips through my fingers again.

I'm jolted awake. A cold sweat trickles down my face. My hair is plastered to my forehead. The glow from the clock reads 2:36 a.m., just like the time before. I turn to my left quietly, but Liv is already awake.

"Same dream?"

"Yeah. You turned to sand this time."

"I guess the beach is out for this year?" she said with a tired smile.

Liv tries to make light of these dreams, but I think deep down they scare her. She hands me a glass of water from the bedside. My mouth tasted like sand, dry and grainy.

"Do you want to talk about it?"

She knew I would say no, but it was nice of her to ask. I've had these dreams ever since Liv and I started dating 5 years ago, every few months like clockwork. Death. Cold sweat. 2:36 a.m.

She nuzzles her head in my chest and quickly falls back to sleep. Sleep is not an option for me tonight. I'll stay up until Liv wakes up the next morning, checking on her breathing every few minutes.

Moving to New York was the best decision I've ever made. It gets a bad rap because back in the day it was pretty shady; but truthfully, I think that's part of the appeal. This is an island of outcasts: the smart ones, the dumb ones, the pretty ones, the weird ones. We're all the same here. We all come from somewhere else looking for the same thing. We weren't accepted where we came from, for one reason or another, so we exiled ourselves to a place where we felt safe amongst the chaos of other misfits. The most interesting and talented individuals end up here and it suddenly becomes desirable to be a part of such an obscure group. The nerds are the popular kids and the popular kids work at a McDonald's in the hometown you left behind. People visit our show all year long just to catch a glimpse of the madness, to feel an ounce of whimsy, but it's lost on them. This is our island. The island of the lost, but for all who dwell here, it's the island of the found.

Before the great move North, I resided below the Mason-Dixon Line, though was never raised a "proper Southerner." My parents were different from their plastic-smiling peers. They grew up in the "flower child" era and never left. Don't get me wrong; they aren't crazy hippies living on patchouli oil and kale. They just have that "all you need is love" attitude. I admire how my parents never hide who they are just to fit in with the PTA moms. Kids are a mosaic of their parents, formed of the good and bad pieces of each parent's personality. Kids are thinkers, carefully analyzing each colorful tile, inspecting it for flaws, testing its strengths and weaknesses. When they grow up and see the spectrum their parents left with them, they choose which parts to take to make them whole. My mosaic was built from two amazing people, but I think there are still a few fragments I need to find on my own.

My father was a farm boy. His family survived off the land, with maybe a rare visit to the local market. They lived a very simple life and wanted for nothing. My grandparents never took my father shopping for toys or clothes outside of major holidays and birthdays. He didn't get anything unless he absolutely needed it. Lucky for him, he was the first child so most of his clothing, toys and books were new. Unfortunately, his younger sister got the hand-me-downs. Each summer before he left for college, my dad would work on the farm picking up pecans, cutting grass and various other farm chores, not for the promise of praise or a meager allowance, but simply because it was what needed to be done. I think that's why my mom and dad fell in love so easily. They both had this unbreakable drive.

My mother grew up very poor and worked hard for every cent. Her childhood home was not much larger than my small one-bedroom apartment in New York and she shared it with her 3 older siblings and parents. She was determined to build a better life than she had growing up. Things we take for granted like clean underwear, fresh linens and sheets were not available to her. She regularly resorted to washing her clothes in the sink and hanging them to dry in the backyard under the hot Virginia sun. Her parents divorced shortly after her seventh birthday, so when it came to relationships, she made sure to get it right the first time.

My mom and dad first met on a blind date set up by a mutual friend. Before Tinder and Match.com, that's how they did it in the old days. My father called my mother promptly after receiving her number on a Thursday evening. Though their conversation was brief, mostly just small talk, they set the date for Friday evening, although which Friday evening was unclear.

The day after their conversation, my mother was sitting in her dorm with no makeup on, in her finest sweatpants, with a bowl of popcorn watching her favorite black and white horror film when she was interrupted by a knock at the door. She peered through the peephole which revealed a heavily bearded man in somewhat outdated clothing holding a bottle of wine. Confused and slightly uncomfortable, she didn't answer the door. He knocked again. She started toward the kitchen to grab whatever weapon she could find to defend herself against this outdated pervert when a realization washed over her and she swung open the door.

"I meant next Friday!" she shouted.

"Oh," he said confused, enjoying the familiar scent of his favorite snack. "Well do you have any popcorn?"

Without skipping a beat, he let himself into her apartment. " 'Psycho!' I love this movie!" he said while making himself comfortable on the couch and tossing a fistful of popcorn into his mouth.

At first, my mother was a little put off, but when she saw the tiny bits of popcorn burrowing their way into his thick beard, she couldn't help but laugh. That night my mother and father met for the first time, sharing a bowl of popcorn, a bottle of wine and hours of conversation. They clicked right away and were engaged six weeks later. Their relationship was one to be envied. They were true partners in life, the yin to each other's yang.

My dad passed away nine years ago from cancer, leaving me to be the "man of the house," as everyone eloquently demanded at his funeral. "Nate, you have to take care of your mother," these faceless men would say in a gruff voice like they were trying to convey their wisdom.

Clearly, they were attempting to convince me that my dreams of studying at NYU were no longer a possibility because my "poor little mother" needed me. If that were the case, I wouldn't need some fair-weather friend of my father's to tell me to stay.

My mother has never been a "poor little" anything. She has never played the victim, even when she had a right to. She is the strongest person I've ever known. At 5-feet,6-inches tall and maybe 130 pounds, she is the only person on this planet who can whoop me into shape without so much as a glare in my direction. She has this quality that makes you want to make her proud. She wants to see you succeed in anything and everything, no matter how crazy it sounds.

So as you can imagine, my mother never asked me to put off my dream of moving to New York to become the cliché struggling artist/college student. It killed her not to have her baby boy around and reminded me of that during our biweekly phone calls, but she knew I was different. I couldn't live in a place where people wore fake smiles and cemented hair, spouting condescending niceties like "bless your heart" or "my, how nice." I needed out.

When I met Liv 5 years later, I knew I was right were I needed to be. I will never forget the first time I saw her. I was in a bar with my college buddies, discussing the deeper things in life like how many girls numbers we could score before 1 a.m., when the silhouette of a girl laughing caught my eye from across the room. Her blond hair was piled on top of her head in a sophisticated mess of waves and knots. I could feel the beat of the music thumping in my chest, but couldn't hear the sound in my ears. Normally, I would have been terrified to walk over to a girl like her, but something pushed me, enlivening me with courage. That something was a good pal of mine named Jack Daniels. I weaved my way through the crowd of gyrating 20-somethings trying desperately not to spill my drink, but before I could get within speaking distance, her eyes caught mine, she smiled, and I ran away like an idiot.

Ten minutes after my epic defeat, I felt a tap on my shoulder. It was the girl. I knew her voice before she spoke a word.

"I was definitely giving you the 'come hither' eyes, but apparently that wasn't working. My feminine wiles must be a little rusty," she said extending her hand out to me. "I'm Liv."

There was no reason we should have met in this sea of people. No reason she should have come up to a plain schmo like me, but she did. From that moment, everything fell right into place. Great apartment, great girl, even my best friend Darrin finally moved up here from North Carolina. Theoretically, my life should have been perfect, but somewhere between my lack of acceptance into the art world after graduation and my need to pay my half of the $2,300 monthly rent, my artistic aspirations dwindled and I resorted to a run-of-the-mill desk job to make ends meet. *It's only until I get my work in a gallery*, I promised myself. *This is temporary*. It wasn't. The more time I spent in the corporate world, the less I painted. A soul-sucking job ran my life and my creativity became fleeting.

There are so many great minds to compete with here; it doesn't seem fair. I was growing further and further away from my dreams, so Liv decided to go out and find some inspiration ... bless her heart.

CHAPTER THREE

Rut

"Liv, I'm not doin' it."

"Nate, just try something different. It will be good for you. You never know, it might open up some inspiration in you. You might find out that you were Michelangelo or something," Liv shouted from the bathroom while brushing her teeth. Laughing slightly too hard at that last comment, I looked up just long enough to catch her eye and quickly did myself a favor by shutting up.

"Are you going to wear your usual 'uniform' today or are you shaking things up in honor of the adventure that you will eventually agree too?" she asked.

My uniform consists of a different variation of the same outfit every day: a pair of actual distressed jeans (not the kind you buy in a store, but the kind you actually fell off your dirt bike and scraped a perfectly tattered hole in), a graphic T-shirt and my well-loved Chuck Taylors. Today's pick was my favorite Ramones T-shirt, gray Chucks and same jeans.

"Should I change?"

"No, you look great! I was just teasing. You know I love your style," she said with a wink.

"Thanks. Anyway, when were you thinking about doing this thing? I mean do you just show up or what? I don't know about …"

"Will you at least go with me? It could be a fun experience even if I am the only one who does it," she said as more of a whine than a question. She was pouting. Damn her and her feminine wiles.

"Okay fine, but I'm not promising that I'll participate. I have enough trouble dealing with things in this life. I don't need to know what happened in the others'. If there are others."

"Some people say that if you know what happened in your past lives, it can clear up problems in your present life. It might not be so bad considering …"

Liv's voice dropped off, but I knew what she was going to say. I'm in a rut, a life rut. We both are. I'm in a rut with my job, with my art, my relationship, everything. I just can't seem to pull myself out of this standstill. I trained at one of the best institutions in the country for aspiring artists and what am I doing? Sitting behind a desk mindlessly calling numbers on an endless spreadsheet selling a tech product I don't even fully understand. Liv trained at Juilliard, arguably THE best school for musicians, and what is she doing? Serving rib eyes to a bunch of rich finance jackasses. Liv tries to liven things up and take advantage of the time we have not consumed by work to jump-start ourselves back into that creative mindset, but nothing has worked so far. It's like a piece of me is waiting to be unlocked, but I can't find the key. Hell, I can't even find the damn lock.

"Come on. We're going to be late if we don't hurry and we don't want to keep Miss Long Legs waiting or she might faint from lack of food intake," Liv said reaching for my hand, pulling me toward the door.

Usually, weekends are pretty standard. Brunch, walking around whichever museum is closest and sketching any one of the masterful pieces of art most New Yorkers take for granted, then finishing the day with a walk around random gallery spaces and meeting up with friends for $5 PBR and shot specials. But lately, our weekends are different.

"We're artists, we're supposed to be uncomfortable. That's what creates art. Do you think Matisse ever said 'Oh yeah, I am super comfortable with that girl's boob on the side of her face'?" Liv asked.

"Matisse didn't put boobs on faces, Liv. He was trying to convey the …"

"I'm going to stop you right there smartass, you know what I mean." Liv was right. I was sketching things that had already been sketched … and painted … and better.

Our first adventure was torturous. With the rise of soft-core S&M novels hitting the market, Liv read about this dominatrix bar called "Chains and Canes" in the Morning Metro and elected me to accompany her there for our Saturday night adventure. What she failed to mention was that you couldn't wear clothes inside the bar. Your outfit had to be checked at the door and you have to enter in nothing but what you were sporting underneath. Sadly for me, it was laundry day.

Liv came prepared in a black lace corset, stockings and a pair of panties that were more like shorts and not at all see-through. I had seen her undress a million times, but never like this. I had to avert my eyes and think about my grandmother playing baseball to avoid the inevitable embarrassment that would come if I let my mind wonder for too long. I, on the other hand, was sporting a white undershirt accented by several small holes, my Avengers boxers, a pair of white Hanes socks, and my nice wingtip dress shoes. I thought Liv was going to pass out laughing.

"Thanks for the heads up."

"I am so sorry!" Liv said practically stumbling over her words with laughter. "I really thought you knew! Didn't you read the email I sent you?"

Oh right, the email with the link I never clicked on. Oops.

Liv slowly peeled back the red velvet curtain, like she was unveiling the newest invention at the World's Fair. We took a full minute to look around, standing in the entrance dumbfounded by the display in front of us. We silently examined every dark corner, every half-naked guy and girl. I looked over at Liv who was composed and calm, while my eyes had to have been twice their normal size. Liv gave me a coy lopsided smile and shrugged.

"No turning back now," she said.

The bar was filled with people of every size, shape, color and age. Women with women, men with men, women with men, women with two men, women with two men wearing collars attached to leashes with ball gags in their mouth. The whole thing reminded me of a scene out of Pulp Fiction, minus the blood.

"That little set will be my souvenir for when you piss me off," Liv said, pulling me to the bar. "What is the appropriate drink for such a spontaneous occasion?"

14

"Beer, for sure. Can't be getting too tipsy or I might let you tie me up on that thing," I said pointing to the wooden X shaped structure in the corner of the bar, which was already occupied by a very enthusiastic trio. The device was as tall as me and had a leather cuff on the end of each plank.

"Only if I can use that on you while you're there." Liv pointed to what looked like a leather riding crop on the wall. I didn't let on, but I actually found the visual extremely sexy.

"Promise?" I jested. Liv playfully shoved me to the side.

The bartender spotted us just as we sat down. "Newbies!" she said enthusiastically. "Welcome! What can I get for you two tonight?"

"Two Brooklyns, please." She looked puzzled by the request. "The lager if you have it on tap?"

A look of realization was followed by what I can only describe as the "bearer of bad news face."

"Oh, I'm afraid we aren't allowed to serve alcohol on the premise. We're a dry bar," she explained.

It was like all the air was sucked out of the room. How could a place like this exist without alcohol? I thought that was the oil that made the machine go.

"We can't have alcohol in here due to lawsuits. Also, it hinders sexual creativity. No one wants a sloppy drunk to hogtie and spank you and then forget how to get you out of it, if you know what I'm sayin'." The woman had a point. That was a quite disturbing image.

"Okay then, lets do a Diet Coke and a Burch beer soda."

As I ordered, my eye caught the glimmer of a shiny silver ring hanging off a pair of ass-less leather chaps worn by a man that had to be at least 68 years old. Beneath the chaps peeked a tiny leather thong with long fringe around the waistband. I tried not to stare, but couldn't help myself. He was on all fours licking the thigh-high boots of a woman dressed in a dominatrix cop outfit. She looked to be about 40 with porcelain skin like you see in old Master paintings. Her face was full and she had a slight roll around her stomach. She was Botticelli's version of an S&M Venus. Her face was pinched into a scowl, her pouty red lips parted ever so slightly, giving orders. She brought the a braided riding crop gently down on the man's rear and placed the ball of her foot on his shoulder.

"Lay down" she commanded in a low authoritative voice. She slowly dragged the fringe of the riding crop over his wrinkled back and snapped it just as she got to his rear. "On the whipping bench." The old man scurried like a frightened church mouse to another medieval looking torture device hiding in a dark corner of the bar and fastened himself to the boards.

"That's Mistress Faye," the bartender said interrupting my trance. "She's a regular. She is usually strictly a female slave mistress, but she has a lot of fun with this one." I looked over at Liv who was as mesmerized as I was. I know it's rude to stare, but in this instance it couldn't be helped. This was the kind of stuff you only see in free porn searches gone wrong, not in the middle of a Manhattan bar.

"These people are just like you," said the bartender. "I see people like you pop in here all the time, just looking for the freak show." Liv opened her mouth to protest, but the bartender cut her off. "You seem like nice people. So are these guys. This is the one place we can be ourselves and not be judged for our fetishes. Nothing illegal or even overly sexual happens here. It's just a place where we can stimulate ourselves. We have all been judged in one relationship or another for our bedroom manner and the rejection hurts, no matter how many times it happens. We have all felt inadequate, like we had some sort of sexual sickness, but here there is nothing wrong with our tastes. We feel safe."

Liv stared at the woman a moment and smiled. "I appreciate you not judging us for our curiosity. Or for his underwear."

Diane Arbus would have had a field day in this place, I thought. A light moan escaped Mistress Faye's latest submissive. Though it sounded painful, the slight smile on his face said otherwise.

"Oh, and Mistress Faye," the bartender said gesturing to the torture scene in front of me, "is an English teacher at a school in the area. And Don over there is the COO at a big financial firm, the name of which I am not at liberty to share with you," she said with a smile and a wink.

They were just like us. They released themselves without fear of failure or judgment. To tell you the truth, I was envious of that kind of exhibitionism. That was the element I needed to channel.

"Cheers to that!" Liv said clinking my glass.

In a bar full of naked people, I was the odd man out and no one even noticed.

On our way to Sunday brunch, Liv and I stopped into the same vintage shop we did every weekend for a reprieve from the summer heat. To the layman, it may look like a pile of junk, but if you look closely, there were thousands of forgotten treasures. Liv could always scope out the oddest trinkets from the masses. She would say, "this feels good," like the object had a pulse.

One afternoon when we first moved into our apartment together, we stumbled upon a second-hand furniture store. The most gorgeous, fluffy white couch was staring at us from the window. It was deep enough to curl up and sleep on, yet long enough that Liv and I would have our own space. Three giant pillows lined the back accented by smaller black, white and blue pillows. The couch sat on carved wooden feet that rose up about three inches off the ground. The fabric was a coarse, yet comfortable canvas that invited you to sink into the cushions and allow it to mold to you. It was perfect.

Liv took one look and completely dismissed it.

"It's just a couch, Liv. How could you have a bad feeling about it?"

"I don't know. I just do."

"Let's just go in and look at it at least. Please?"

Liv was silent, staring at the couch, until she finally lifted her head and nodded toward the entrance.

"She's a beauty," the sales clerk said, showing us over to the couch in the window. "Got her in yesterday. Some lady moved here from Alabama and couldn't fit it in her studio. You wouldn't believe how many people have stopped in to take a look."

I touched the tough fabric encompassing the back cushions, crunching it with my hand, feeling the goose down mold to me and spring back. Instinctively, I jumped onto the couch and sprawled out.

"Come on, try it Liv," I said, patting the seat next to me. Hesitantly, she sat down like she was sitting on a bed of nails. "Comfy, right?" She nodded and shrugged her shoulders.

"It's okay, I guess. How much is it?" Liv asked, eyeing the clerk.

"$400," he replied.

"$400! That's it!" I was shocked. This couch could easily go for $1,500 used.

"Yeah, there are a few brown spots if you look closely. Someone spilled a whole lot of something on here. It looks like they got most of it up, but you can see the light shadows of some of the spills."

"Well that's gross," I said quickly removing myself from the couch.

"Such a shame, too. It's an awesome couch. Old, but in great shape."

"Do you have anything ..." But before I could finish, I spotted Liv sprawled out on a gigantic brown leather chair in the middle of the store. She looked so cozy. Her strawberry golden hair spilling over her wool coat, long legs swung over the side like she had sat in that chair a million times. It was made for her.

"Nate, if you were a chair I think you would be this one."

"So, I guess that means we will be buying the chair." Her eyes grew wide and a cautious smile consumed her face in the most awkward way.

"How much for this one?" I asked, turning to the clerk.

"This one is $350 and it doesn't have any spots," the clerk said, trying to make at least one sale today.

"We'll take it!" She grabbed my hand and we walked out with a lovely chair, leaving what would later be known as "the karma couch" behind. The funny thing is, as beautiful and magnificent as that couch was, it still sits in the window years later.

"Nate! I found something."

"Of course you did. Soon we are going to run out of space for your random finds. We do live in a New York City apartment and not a big one."

"Oh, come on party pooper. It's very small."

"Okay, what is it?" I half expected another porcelain figurine of a Japanese cat or something equally as cheesy like other objects she insisted on filling the house with, but to my surprise it wasn't. It was a large embossed brass button. I examined the button and rubbed my thumb over the raised seal. It almost looked like a coat of arms. The texture felt strangely familiar, even comforting. The image was an eagle with its wings out stretched and a shield with the letters C.S.A. across it.

"I wonder what 'CSA' stands for? Crusty Sandwich Alert?" Clearly my mind was on food.

"I love it. It will look awesome on my old winter coat with the mismatched buttons. So it won't take up any extra space. Liv said with a glare. "How much?"

"One dollar."

Liv handed the clerk a dollar for the button and placed it in her purse.

"Isn't it weird to think that someone could have worn this button every day? I mean think about it. Whoever this button belonged to, that person's energy lives in that object," Liv said, successfully hinting at today's upcoming events.

"Well then you better hope he wasn't a serial killer, otherwise we're screwed" I taunted. Liv elbowed me playfully and took my arm as we walked down the street toward our brunch spot.

CHAPTER FOUR

Darrin Edgars

"Well it's about damn time y'all!" Darrin shouted as soon as we entered the restaurant.

He was hard to miss and his voice was just as rousing, but Darrin was used to having all eyes on him. Standing at six-foot-five with muscles bursting out of his shirt, he is a strikingly handsome African-American man with a panty-dropping Southern accent. In college, he was the top defensive lineman in the ACC for North Carolina State.

"Liv had to stop at Times 2 and you know how hard it is to get her out of there. You can blame her for our tardiness," I said. Liv shot me the eye-roll to end all eye-rolls. It was so dramatic, I thought she might fall over. "Anyway D, what's up?" I said as Liv made the round of hugs to Darrin and his new girlfriend, Rae.

Rae was your typical wanna-be model Manhattan party girl. Long, stick-straight brown hair, unrealistic tan, and so thin you would think her legs would snap on top of her sky-high heels. Her hobbies included constant at-rest-bitch-face and staring into her iPhone for hours to keep up with all of the A-list celebrities on Instagram, Twitter, Facebook and every other social media platform. And let's not forget about the endless train of selfies. In reality, her given name is Raquel, which she later shortened to "Rae," in an attempt to hide her Jewish heritage, which was soon completely erased by the nose job she was undoubtedly given on her 18th birthday, in true New York socialite fashion.

"I hope we didn't keep you waiting too long," I said, hoping to smooth over our late entrance.

"Nah, we were just ordering drinks," Darrin responded.

Darrin Edgars has been my best friend since he took a punch in the eye for me from the school bully in kindergarten. I was a scrawny kid when I was young, always sat in the front of the bus with the geeks. Billy, a monstrous first-grader, used to take pleasure in pulling the glasses off my face and screaming "Nerd!" as he walked with the other cool kids to the back of the bus. Super original on Billy's part.

Well, one cool November morning, I had had enough. I picked my glasses up off the bus floor, looked Billy right in the eye and said, "Fuck you." I had first heard the word used on TV when the babysitter was over on mom and dad's date night. That night, I had decided that my 8 p.m. bedtime was unacceptable for a child of my intellect, so I snuck out of bed and watched the TV from the balcony overlooking the living room, completely under the radar; a true rebel through and through. As soon as the person on TV said those words, the babysitter gasped, so I knew it was bad.

The bus fell silent. Billy's face turned 30 shades of red.

He reared up his fist like one of the Three Stooges, swinging it in circles behind his head. I winced, ready to receive my punishment, but it never came. Darrin had stepped in front of me and taken one right in the eye. It must not have hurt that bad, because he still had the strength to kick Billy square in the balls. Needless to say, Billy never messed with us again and Darrin and I have been best friends ever since.

Darrin and I grew up down the street from each other in the suburbs of Richmond until I decided to leave for college at NYU and Darrin got a football scholarship to North Carolina State. Football was Darrin's life and art was mine. We were always so different in so many ways, even in the way we look. It is almost comical watching us walk down the street together. People will stare at Darrin because of his towering size, which is only highlighted by having the scrawniest white guy ever walk next to him, but he never minded. Darrin lived for the spotlight. Even when we were in high school, he would drag me into every school talent show, play and pep rally. He loved a crowd and the crowd loved him. I remember our final talent show performance during our senior year in high school. Darrin dragged me into a particularly embarrassing act where I dressed up like a girl with a large rear while he rapped Sir Mix-A-Lot's "Baby Got Back." He killed it with his smooth dance moves and well-rehearsed rapping, while I provided the pillow-filled comedic rump shaking.

That being said, Darrin isn't a self-centered guy. He doesn't come off as cocky or rude, but rather fun-loving and confident. Even through all of his accomplishments and accolades, he has managed to stay humble with his feet on the ground. He has never missed even one of my art openings, no matter how small. Even if he had to fly up to New York, he was always there to support me. We've always had each other's backs.

When Darrin got a job up here with ESPN last year, we were right back to old high school Nate and D. Even though he came up to visit often and I came back for holidays and a few of his football games, it was never the same as being able to call him up to hang out like the old days. It just feels right, him being here.

"So what are y'all up to this weekend? Any more amazing adventures to the bondage bar?" Even though Darrin has lived up here for about a year now, he never quite lost his accent. Lucky for me, mine only comes out when I drink.

"Well, Liv has this brilliant idea that we are going to some psychic to 'read our past lives'," I explained.

"O.M.G you have to do it," Rae piped up. I don't think I've heard her say more than three words before, but apparently this struck a nerve. "My sister's boyfriend's cousin is super into that stuff and she found out so much about herself by doing it. She went to this lady who was, like, a legit doctor and she did, like, the hypnosis and everything. She said it was totally life-changing." Now I see why Darrin didn't let her talk. She's an idiot.

"Dude, I think that sounds awesome. What if you were like Elvis or something?"

"Then I would have met an untimely death way too soon, so I kind of hope that's not the case." The waitress came by and sat three mimosas and a glass of green juice that looked like Gak in front of us.

"That looks awful, what is it?" I said, feeling my face turn in disgust.

Rae springs up, "It's kale, spinach, lemon and apple juice. I'm on a cleanse." Of course she is.

"Anyway Liv, I think that's a sick idea. I would love to know who I was in my past life. I feel like I was someone epic, like Jay Z," Darrin said.

"D, you couldn't have been Jay Z, he is still alive," I respond, attempting to poke enough holes in his logic to get me out of this charade.

"Whatever dude, you know what I mean. Do you even have a reason for not wanting to go? I mean really what could it hurt? Liv has to put up with you every day," Darrin said nudging me with his shoulder. I spot Liv out of the corner of my eye trying to hide the smirk that is about to eclipse her face. Then I thought about it. I had no reason for not wanting to go. Maybe it was my stubborn stance and general aversion to anything supernatural, but there was no reason I couldn't do this for Liv if it would help her to access her creativity. There was no getting out of this one.

"So, what do you say? Will you do it?" There is something about Liv that can convince you to do anything.

"Okay fine. But if I was Lex Luther in my previous life, you can't hold it against me," I said, begrudgingly.

"Okay, deal."

CHAPTER FIVE
Dr. Cecilia Rose, MD

Before I could even shake Liv's hand to make our "deal" official, we scarfed down brunch and practically ran to our next destination.

"Are you sure we're in the right place?" I asked Liv.

The lobby was warm, almost elegant, decorated with oversized leather couches and chairs with inviting pillows. The walls were lined with a mixture of famous impressionist and surrealist prints. I would have never placed the two together, but surprisingly, it worked. The colors were brilliant. I recognized one of the prints immediately, a painting by Manet, "Girl with a Parrot." I don't know why, but I've always felt there was more to this painting than the artist portrayed, like he was shrouding this young woman in mystery by making her look so ordinary. The simplicity is eerie in comparison with his other works. The subjects were always dignified and alive with color. This girl looked like a commoner thrown into a painting with seemingly random objects and a pet parrot. I wrote a paper about it in college, probably the only one I really enjoyed writing. Apparently, my professor did not agree with my hypothesis, because he gave me a C saying I "hadn't really understood the artist's intentions."

"Are you here to see Dr. Rose?" said a woman who materialized from the doorway to our left. She was dressed in a long hippie-like skirt with a geometric design accompanied by a billowy white blouse that practically swallowed her small frame. Her petite face was overtaken by a genuine smile. She seemed way too peppy to be at work on a Sunday. She resembled a young Yoko Ono, but with less angst. The only thing she was missing was a daisy and a pair of round, tinted sunglasses.

"Yes, we have an appointment at 2? We're a little early," Liv said. I could tell she was trying to withhold her excitement.

"Great! Take a seat. She will be with you shortly. Can I get you all anything in the meantime? Water? Tea?"

"No, thank you! We're fine," Liv answered nervously.

"Well, my name is Shelly. I will be right through this door if you need anything!" she said, exiting through the door behind her.

Liv and I sat on the brown leather couch closest to the door. She was squeezing my hand so hard I thought she might break it. I could feel her nerves as I watched her chew habitually on the right side of her lip, like she did before every performance. What did she think was going to happen in there?

A middle-aged woman dressed in a pinstripe pantsuit approached us from the same door. She had her graying blond hair tucked into neat bun at the nape of her neck. Not a hair was out of place. Her large green eyes peered over a pair of rectangular reading glasses, acknowledging us with a welcoming smile as she looked up from her clipboard.

"Ah, Mr. James, Ms. Hammond, welcome," she said in a slight British accent, extending her hand to us individually. "Please, follow me into my office." She didn't wear a turban or weird crystal jewelry. She looked more like a shrink than a psychic.

Dr. Rose's office had a spread of tea and lemon water with small snacks. She eyed me staring at them.

"Food and drink put the body at ease. It makes my patients feel more comfortable during our sessions. Please, help yourselves." I had just eaten, but the sight of free food made me feel ravenous, so I took a heaping plate of cookies and a tall glass of the lemon water. "So, you finally got him to come around I see," said Dr. Rose.

"Yes, it took some convincing, right up to the last minute actually, but he's here," Liv responded.

"Wonderful. Well sit and let me explain the process to you before we begin."

I took a seat on the couch next to Liv, stuffing my face with the most delightful butter cookies. Some had sprinkles, some were dipped in dark chocolate with coconut shavings. Even if I wasn't excited about whatever this is, it was definitely worth going for the cookies and fancy water. I was already plotting how I could slip some into Liv's purse without anyone noticing.

"I know you probably have questions about how this works, so I will explain the process and set expectations before we begin. I am getting an energy off of you, Ms. Hammond, which means we can do this while you are awake. It shouldn't be too hard to open you up. Basically, I will be seeing the lives you have lived and relaying them to you secondhand. I may see one life, I may see more. The thing to remember is that I am only being shown pieces of the lives that will aid you in achieving your highest good in this lifetime.

"Nathan you are a bit closed off, as I suspected you might be. For you, I suggest placing you into a meditative state. This way we will really be able to penetrate the metaphysical wonderland you have stored in that soul of yours."

"Does that mean I literally get to sleep through this?" *Now, that I could get into.* After last night, I could use some shuteye.

"You will be in an alternate state of consciousness, but you will not be asleep. Your body will most likely feel refreshed when you awaken, but mentally you may feel a little exhaustion," Dr. Rose explained. That didn't sound too bad. All I had to do was lay there and think.

"I do have to give you a few warnings about the regression so you know what to expect. When you go into your meditative state, you won't be able to control the actions of your past self. It is like a dream in the way it feels, but you can't determine where it will go, like you are following the lead of your own mind. You may see yourself do things that you would not do now, think things you find repulsive, but you cannot stop it. These actions have already happened. They have shaped your soul and brought you to where you are today. Throughout the process, I will be asking questions that you will answer based on what you see. You may or may not hear my voice within this dreamlike state, but your brain will register my questions and you will answer. For some of my clients, this has been too much and they have suffered panic attacks and other mentally-induced reactions from the stress, so I need to convey the risks before we move forward."

"I think I will be able to handle it," I said, cockily. How bad could it really be? Definitely not worse than the dreams I am already having.

"Some people observe these lives through the eyes of their past self, living in their head, hearing their thoughts and yours at the same time. Others observe from outside of the body, like watching a film. Sometimes it is a combination of the two. I will need you to sign these release papers before we can begin. An EMT is on site at all times in case of severe exhaustion or if you experience a panic attack."

I signed the papers without hesitation. This is ridiculous. *An EMT on site? Really?*

"Okay, just a few questions before we start,"Dr. Rose said collecting the papers and placing them on her desk." Typically, someone will only see the past lives that are relative to what will help them in this life's journey. What are you both looking to achieve through this regression?"

Liv and I looked at each other, unprepared for this question.

"Honestly, I just feel lost," Liv said without prompting. Her voice was small, almost embarrassed. "I don't know where my life is going or what my passion is anymore. I used to think it was music, but lately I just feel like I have lost my lust for it. I feel really broken down by the stress of life and my creativity has definitely taken a hit. I feel almost lazy and am unable to pull myself out of it." Her head was cowering toward her shoulders like she was ashamed. I knew she was feeling this way, but I had no idea it was having this kind of effect on her. She looked so sad. "I didn't know all of that was going to come out," she said with an embarrassed smile.

"Sometimes you just need to be asked the hard questions to elicit a true answer," Dr. Rose said encouragingly. "And how about you, Nathan?"

"Me, too. I mean, I feel that way also," was all I could string together.

"Okay, we can definitely work with that. I have a lot of clients that come to me during a crossroads or lost point in their lives. Ms. Hammond, if you're ready, we can begin with you. Mr. James, would you like to stay and watch?"

Liv looked at me, her eyes wide. "I'll stay," I said, grabbing Liv's hand.

"And we're off!"

"It's started already?" Liv gasped.

"When Nate touched your hand, you lit up like a Christmas tree, your aura I mean. This typically indicates a strong past life connection, though I can't confirm it until I regress Nate.

"The scene is set in what looks to be around the Civil War era. You have long dark hair. You are sitting in a chair holding an infant. There is a tall young man standing behind you, tickling you and the child. It looks like you two are married, newlyweds even. You both can't be older than 22. The man straightens up and looks ahead, along with you. You both look like you are trying not to smile. There is a flash of light. I believe this is your family portrait. You both stay still even after the flash, but it's apparent you are trying to contain laughter. It's quite a comical scene, actually," Dr. Rose said with a slight chuckle.

"The scene is changing now. You look sad and

disheveled, like you haven't slept in days. You're holding this old piece of paper, perhaps a letter. You keep running your fingers over the words. Tears are starting to roll down your face. I can hear the baby crying in another room. You curl into a ball on the floor, covering your ears, rocking back and forth. Do you happen to keep greeting cards, Christmas cards, any sort of written correspondence?"

"She has a scrapbook full of them divided by type of card, date, and who they came from," I chimed in. "It's pretty intense."

"You did this in your past life, also. There are stacks of them everywhere. They look like love letters. The one you were holding looks like it is signed with 'Love Always and Forever, J.' Your tears are beginning to stain the pages. You start to gently dab them away, careful not to smear the calligraphy.

"There is a knock from somewhere, the front door. You open the door and immediately hug the visitor. This is a different man from the one in the previous scene. This man has a thick beard and wide blue eyes. He looks very similar to your past self. He is carrying a weight in his eyes I can't quite place. He hands you something, a locket I think. You collapse into the visitor's arms, weeping. He picks you up and carries you into a bedroom. I can still hear the baby crying in the other room. He puts you under the covers and places the locket around your neck. The visitor is saying, 'He asked that you never forget him. He wanted me to make sure I gave this to you. I was with him until the end. It was peaceful. His last thoughts were of you and John. You can't give up, Lucy. Don't let this destroy you. I was relieved of my duties and came home to help you through this. I am always here for you, sister.'"

I turned to face Liv. Tears have pooled in her eyes, but she didn't let them escape. I grasped her hand tighter.

"The gentleman got up and retrieved the child from another room. He looks to be older than in the previous scene, maybe 1 or 2 years old. The man, your brother I assume, tries to hand him to you. You refuse. 'I can't bear it. He looks too much like him. I can hardly look at him,' you say. Your brother is staring at you, his face is hardened now. 'You will not let him down, Lucy. I made him a promise and I intend to keep it.' He hands you the baby again, very gently, laying him on your chest. You embrace the baby, hesitantly at first, and then enveloping him with your arms. He stops crying almost immediately. The baby is looking right into your face, his eyes glistening, and smiles so wide it's contagious. You are thinking he is lucky to have his father's smile, the smile you loved so much. You smile back and kiss the baby on the forehead. The love you feel is overwhelming and you start to cry, your tears rolling onto his cheeks. Your brother is smiling, watching the two of you. He feels like he has kept his promise to his friend, your husband."

Liv's breathing regulates from her silent cries and a familiar smile invades her face. I remove my hand from hers to place it around her shoulders.

"That is all I have been given at this moment," said Dr. Rose. "Does any of this resonate with anything you are feeling or experiencing in your current life?"

Liv took a moment to think, but I could tell her mind was flying, like it does when she composes. Like she is in some sort of alternate world she built for herself.

"Nothing that comes to mind. I have never experienced

anything that ... devastating."

"Allow yourself time to think. Place this experience in the back of your mind for now and allow life to happen around you," Dr. Rose said, scribbling down a few notes. "It may come to you later when you are least expecting it."

Liv still had that look on her face. Her mind was still somewhere else. "But, is that it? I was expecting to find something that would help me in this life. I feel even more lost than I did before, trying to make sense of all this."

"For now, yes, that's all they have given me. There is a reason you were shown that particular life and those particular events. It is very clear to me that you have lived many lives, so I am sure you have no shortage of journeys to pull from, but this was the one chosen. It may not be clear now, but take some time to reflect on her actions, her feelings and her shortcomings. It will become clearer for you. Remember, the point of past life regression is to aid you in achieving your highest good in this life."

Liv didn't seem to be reassured by Dr. Rose's explanation, but she nodded her head and continued to drift into her own thoughts.

"If it is of any comfort, it is very clear that you and Mr. James have a strong connection, which I can only attribute to you being in each other's lives for many lifetimes. They have been hounding me to regress him since your arrival. I think before I can give you any more, they will need to show Mr. James a thing or two."

"Who is 'they'?" I knew what she was going to say. I don't even know why I asked.

"The Masters, your spiritual guides. They know you aren't exactly open to the experience and they are eager to get in touch with you." She looks up from her scribbles right at me, like I called her name.

"There is a piece of you missing, Mr. James. You have been trying to fill it with work, money and things. They're all distractions. Let's find that missing piece, shall we?" Dr. Rose gestured to the empty end of the couch. Liv got up and moved to a chair nearby. "Please, lay down Mr. James. Make yourself comfortable."

CHAPTER SIX

Resistance

I'm not a religious person. I don't believe in every aspect of the Bible like my Southern Baptist peers and I don't believe that positive attendance dictates your eligibility into to heaven, if there is such a place. Perhaps we just die, and that's it. No white light, no outer body experience, just death. Just inevitable oblivion. Maybe believing in an afterlife is just a trick we play on ourselves so we don't spend our lives fearing what comes next.

My life altering religious experiences have been limited, to say the least. I have no reason to take solace in a God who has never shown Himself during my life. In fact, when I did blindly believe, my life fell apart, one domino toppling the next until I finally left it behind. When my father died, I was not given some reassuring sign that everything would be okay, that he would be at peace in his final destination. I got nothing but unforgiving pain. The kind of pain that lives deep inside you, so deep that sometimes you think it's finally gone, but it was just sleeping, laying low, waiting to creep back into view at a moment's notice. I realize these things happen in life and I don't blame God for my misfortune, but a little reassurance would have been nice. Now I am lying on a couch letting some whack job get into my head and access my "past lives." Dr. Rose is not God, but maybe she can provide me with more closure than He did, even if it is bullshit.

"Let's do this. How do we start?" I said, eager to close my eyes for a while.

Dr. Rose lit something on fire and waved it around the room.

"It's just sage. I'm cleansing the air around you. You carry a lot of negativity. It attracts undesirable spirits during our session because your soul is exposed, metaphorically, of course. Sage cleanses the room and gives us all a clear and open mind."

"Negative energy? I am the happiest guy I know!" I exclaimed.

"Are you, Mr. James?"

Dr. Rose's question took me by surprise. I have never admitted it to myself, because no one had ever asked me that question so blatantly, but I wasn't happy, not about where my life was going. I felt it every day a little bit more, the unhappiness creeping in. It affected my work, my social life, my relationship, my art. The only thing that made me happy lately was when I was with Liv and Darrin. When I'm alone, it's just me with my thoughts. I wasn't happy. I was defeated.

"Let's just get this over with," I said, waving off her question.

"Alright then. Ms. Hammond, I am going to ask you to stay in the far corner of the room. Mr. James, are you comfortable?"

"Yeah, feelin' good, Doc."

Dr. Rose dimmed the lights and played some soft hippy-dippy music. I'm a little embarrassed to say this, but I kind of liked it.

"Close your eyes. Take your mind to somewhere safe, a favorite place. Keep yourself in that peaceful place." Dr. Rose's voice dropped about two octaves. How cliché. *This is ridiculous.* "Take a deep breath, hold it for three counts and exhale. Feel yourself sinking deeper and deeper into the couch. Allow your toes to wiggle and relax." I felt myself relaxing without trying. It felt good.

"Now allow your legs to fall heavy and relax ... your torso falls into the couch, relaxed ... wiggle your fingers and let them fall limp ... your shoulders and arms following, falling heavy on the couch ... your neck holds no weight. Your head falls heavy on the pillow. Your body is completely relaxed. Allow yourself become weightless ... sinking deeper and deeper into relaxation. With each breath, you sink deeper. Stay in that beautiful place in your mind."

I'm in my tree on my grandparent's farm. It's a large weeping willow with lots of sturdy branches, perfect for climbing. We stayed there during the summer months to help my grandparents with farm chores as they got older. I spent hours just daydreaming in that tree, making up stories and drawing imagined creatures. I haven't been back there in years, but I know this is where I can remember being the happiest.

"Imagine a white light coming down into the crown of your head ... now push the light into your chest, illuminating your organs, all the way down through your feet. You are encompassed by this safe white light … now imagine a path. It can be a path you know or a path you simply see in front of you. Begin to walk that path. The path is safe, you are safe … what do you see coming up ahead of you?"

I envision the trail that led into the woods behind my childhood home. My father used to play with me on this path. We would pretend to be knights searching for the enemies' hidden quarters or cowboys and Indians. It was always safe because he was there, fighting off the bad guys, making sure nothing got me. Up ahead I see darkness, but I wasn't afraid. I walk into the dark. I can feel something there, I'm curious.

"Do you know…" Dr. Rose's voice is slipping away. The world goes black.

CHAPTER SEVEN

The War of Northern Aggression

The ringing in my ears is unbearable. A strong blast rang out from what felt like two yards away. I slowly open my eyes to a world founded in chaos. A dusty brown haze lies on top of my body like a thick blanket. I try to move my right arm, one finger at a time. It works. Then my left. That works, too. Just as I begin to lift my torso off the ground, I feel a strong hand push me backward. Slowly my eyes begin to focus on a gray figure in in the fog. He turns to me, bringing his face inches from mine, screaming, "Stay down, Jack! They done advanced us!"

He was a scraggly man in a mess of a gray suit with dense facial hair in his early twenties. His eyes were focused and unwavering as he loaded what looked like an old rifle. He ripped open a small pouch with his teeth and poured a black powder into the muzzle, packing it down with a long metal rod, then settled the butt of the archaic gun into the crook of his shoulder and pulled the trigger. His shoulder jumped back from the recoil. Without realizing it, my hand had traveled to a small round button on my jacket. I was rubbing it consistently clockwise, like it was holding me to the ground. I rolled my head to the right. There was a canon on two large wheels armed by three men.

"Fire in the hole!" The third man lit the fuse on the back end of the canon and an earth-shattering boom sent my heart into my stomach. I winced at the roar of the canon, rolling back upright. Suddenly, two large hands grabbed me from my underarms and pull me into a trench.

"Hang in there, Jack. They say it's almost over."

The words took a minute to find their way through his ears and into my brain. I felt disoriented, like everything was happening in slow motion. I propped my back up against the wall of the trench. My hand pressed into something cold and fleshy. I turned and lifted my hand to get a good look. It was a body – a dead body – of a young boy holding a small drum. His eyes were glazed over with a milky white film. His skin was void of color save for the blood speckled just beneath his chin. I gazed down the trench. It was lined with dead bodies in gray suits. But they weren't suits. They were more like uniforms. I looked down at my hand, still subconsciously rubbing the button on my uniform. C.S.A. It was just like the one Liv bought from the vintage shop. "Confederate States of America" appeared in my mind like a blinking answer on a game show. I was a soldier of the Confederate Army.

I let the realization wash over me, trying to convince myself that this man couldn't have been me. I was back in the very place I had tried so hard to escape. These narrow-minded values and uptight traditions were something I actually fought to uphold at some point in my endless existence … or did I? What if this is just something I am imagining? But why this? Why would I imagine the Civil War? *Wake up, Nate … Wake up! No dice.*

I climbed to my feet amongst the bodies in the trench, careful not to step on one.

"Here," said the man who had pulled me into the trench, now holding another rifle.

"What year is it?" I was wondering this question in my head but it came out uncontrollably. My name is Jackson. I just saw it appear in my head. I could feel Jackson was disoriented. His thoughts were everywhere.

"Shit, Jack, I didn't know I hitcha that hard! Musta knocked the wind right outtya."

"Why did you hit me?"

"Well it was my fist or a Yankee bullet between your eyes."

"You saved me?"

"Jack, we always gonna look out for each other, here and forever. Just like when we was kids." Then he winked at me with a smug smile.

There was something so familiar about the man. I felt an unshakable bond of brotherhood I had only found with one other person – Darrin. It was him, it had to be. But instead of taking a punch from the school bully, he was knocking me out of the line of fire. I hear another large blast ring out from behind me.

"Here, Goddammit! We need you, Jackson!"

I grabbed the rifle and my hands did the rest, like I was on autopilot. I watched my hands lift a package of black powder from a small pouch I was wearing on my right side, which I hadn't noticed until now. My mouth tore the top of package, spitting the trash onto the ground. It tasted metallic and dusty. A drop of blood stained the packaging. I poured the coarse black powder into the muzzle and packed it as I had seen my friend do before. Automatically, I pulled the rifle to my shoulder and settled it into the space between my shoulder and chest, where Liv usually lays her head to fall asleep. Jackson aimed the muzzle at a blurry navy figure in the distance and pulled the trigger. A second later, the figure dropped to the ground.

"When Lee ends up givin' you some kinda medal for being the best damn marksman in the Confederate Army, don't be lettin' your head get too big. I did save your ass," he said nudging me with his elbow, a gesture that felt all too familiar.

Jackson's thoughts began to run lucid through my mind. I saw his life in a matter of seconds and everything clicked. Jackson began reloading his rifle.

"How's the leg?" Nelson asked.

Nelson was the man's name. I followed Nelson's gaze down to Jackson's right leg. A large wound in the middle of his thigh was wet with blood.

"It hurts, but I think the bullet passed all the way through." The words just flew out of my mouth. I felt like a puppet being worked by a ventriloquist.

Jackson had been shot, but he was not letting on to how much pain he was in. His pain ran rampant though my mind, though I couldn't physically feel its sting.

"Well them Yanks are almost done for, so we can gittcha back to the tent and have the medic take a look."

Jackson loaded his gun 147 more times and took 143 more Union lives. As I watched my hands pull the trigger on another life, I silenced my thoughts and listened to his. With each shot, Jackson's mind was clear. He had no sorrow, no regret for the lives he had taken. He was a machine, picking off one man at a time. One word appeared in Jackson's mind throughout that gruesome afternoon: Home. That is all he thought about. That was his motivation.

Jackson's right leg was starting to go numb just as I saw the Union begin their retreat. I could feel him slipping out of consciousness. All I could hear beyond the ringing in my ears was the celebratory Rebel Yell. Jackson grabbed for Nelson's arm, falling to the ground beside him. His eyes closed. I'm shut out.

I feel a shift; it's as if I was on a trampoline and was double-bounced into the air, but never hit the ground. I open my eyes to find myself standing over Jackson, this time outside of his body. Jackson was laid out on a cot inside a freestanding tent just beyond the outskirts of the battlefield. There were at least 300 cots holding men with injuries of all sorts and even more men laying on the grass bleeding. Some had bandages around their heads, and some with bloody stumps for hands and feet. Some just looked dead. The cots were stained red, yellow and brown. I could see some men's wounds being wrapped, while others were openly operated on. A symphony of painful screams from every direction filled the stale air. Nelson leaned over Jackson, examining his wounds alongside someone who looked to be the Confederate doctor.

"But the bullet went straight through! Shouldn't he be alright?" Nelson sounded desperate.

"The wound has had time to fester; it's infected. He was out there too long on the battlefield," said the medic.

The doctor wore a long coat, that I imagine at one point was white, but is now splattered with bodily fluids. His face was smeared with blood that was obviously not his own. His eyes were dark and tired, like he hadn't slept in days. Jackson looked straight toward the sky, not at the doctor or at Nelson, tuning them out to listen to his own thoughts, which I could still hear, even though we no longer shared a physical body. He was worried. Not for his life, but for the family he would leave behind.

"Take the leg," said Jackson. Nelson stared at his friend like he was a madman.

"No! I will not allow this! I told my sister I would take care of you and I will not bring you home to her missin' a damn limb!" They weren't friends. They were brothers. It made more sense every moment I spent in this weird world.

"It's that or you'll be bringin' me home in a box. Take your pick."

"We used up the last of the anesthesia on the first wave of injuries, so we are going to have to do this the old fashioned way," said the doctor. "I will give you a minute to get liquored up, then we'll start." The doctor handed Jackson a brown jug that smelled like paint thinner. He flinched in disgust as he took a long pull from the jug. Jackson tilted the bottle toward Nelson.

"You're gonna need this as much as I do."

Hesitantly, Nelson took the bottle from Jackson and took a small sip from the jug and handed it back to Jackson. Jackson took two more large gulps, his face fighting his repulsion to the bitter taste.

I turned my attention to Nelson who was staring right at me, like he could see me. I walked closer to him, waving my hands inches from his face, but it wasn't me he was staring at blankly. He was staring through me. His eyes looked hollow and sad. I turned around and immediately wished I hadn't. In front of me was a gigantic pile of severed limbs. Legs, feet, arms, hands. Tossed away like old chicken bones from last night's dinner.

I looked to my right, and there was the battlefield. Smoke still hung in the air from the thousands of shots fired that day. The ground was littered with the bodies of dead soldiers. A mixture of gray and blue suits stained with red as far as the eye could see. It was hard to tell who had actually won the battle.

I forced my mind to try to pinpoint the exact battle. Letters and sounds started to appear jumbled in my mind, like a toddler sounding out their first word. But one word was very clear. *Virginia*. I felt a shiver run through my body. This place had felt familiar since the moment I opened my eyes in Jackson's mind.

It's very likely that I had been here before. Growing up in Virginia, the Civil War is what Richmond was known for: the capital of the Confederacy. We have a whole avenue of statues dedicated to every significant general in the war, and Arthur Ashe of course. We couldn't have a whole avenue full of monuments to white Confederates without breaking it up a little! That would just be racist... In grade school, they dragged us to every battle site within 100 miles, retelling the same stories about the same men who were the same great, great, great grandfathers of the same families who run the city.

I walked deeper into the battlefield, hoping it could

provide some context as to which battle I witnessed … or fought in … or both. I reached the edge of the battlefield, but something stopped me, like I ran into a closed glass door. I looked up, but there was nothing there. I pushed against the invisible object, but it wouldn't budge. Dr. Rose did say that I couldn't change anything.

"How ya feelin', Jack?" I heard Nelson ask behind me.

"Like the time we broke into your daddy's good liquor when we were kids and got a proper ass whoopin'," said Jackson trying to laugh.

His eyelids were beginning to droop, like he could barely keep them open. The pupils of his eyes were darting around the tent, desperate to cling to something still, fighting the moonshine to stay awake. A serious look invaded Nelson's brief smile.

"I think we're ready, Doc," Nelson said motioning to Jackson.

"Wait." Jackson reached into his pocket and pulled what looked like a locket and placed it in Nelson's hand. "Give it back to her," he said. "She gave it to me for luck before I left and I promised that I would give it back to her when I returned."

Nelson opened the charm and inside was a black and white photograph of a family. The woman had dark, wavy hair pulled back into a long braid seated in a wooden dining chair holding a baby. Jackson stood behind them, his left hand laid gently on the woman's shoulder, staring out into the distance. It looked like the couple was trying to repress a smile, though their eyes were unmistakably shining through their straight faces.

The woman looked like no one I had ever seen before, but familiar at the same time. I looked closer. Her eyes smiled the same way Liv's do. It was her, unmistakably. Just like I had recognized Darrin, Liv was staring back at me from another time. I could feel Jackson aching at the thought of leaving them. Inside his head, the thought of leaving his family was more excruciating than the shooting pains in his leg. I saw his tear, but I could feel it roll down my cheek.

"If this is lucky, then you need it, not me." Nelson took the locket from his hand and placed it around his neck. Without hesitation, Nelson dropped to his knees beside Jackson's cot, his head resting in his hands, praying silently. When he finished, he gave the doctor a woeful nod and squeezed Jackson's hand. If this were to happen to Darrin and me in real life, he would have clarified this action with "no homo dude." But Nelson was not ashamed, which surprised me.

"Go on, Doc," instructed Jackson.

The doctor handed Nelson a long stick, just wide enough to separate Jackson's jaw. Instinctively, Nelson placed it in Jackson's mouth as he bit down. Nelson held the two ends of the stick behind Jackson's head, preparing to hold it in place as the doctor began.

The next ten minutes were agonizing to watch. I felt Jackson's hands latch on to Nelson's arms as he held the bite stick, his nails digging into Nelson's skin as the bone saw rocked back and forth. I could hear the ripping of flesh, then into something tougher. Jackson's screams were piercing, even through his clenched jaw. His pain pulsated though my mind. I could hardly think. I could not feel the physical pain of what Jackson was feeling, only what was going on in his mind, which was just as terrifying. His eyes were wide as he looked back at Nelson, begging him to take the pain away. Nelson watched Jackson writhe in pain, helpless to stop his agony. After what seemed like an hour, I hear the familiar grinding sound of sawing. The doctor had hit bone.

After two long minutes, Jackson's thoughts fell silent. I could only hear my thoughts now. Jackson had finally passed out from the pain. Blood spilled onto the sheets as the doctor continued to saw, wiping his brow every so often, caked with the humidity of the day. I watched a few droplets of his sweat spill into Jackson's open wound while he was working and suddenly found a new appreciation for the cleanliness of modern medicine. I have never seen so much blood in my life. The doctor pulled the tourniquet tighter to try to stop the bleeding. It slowed, but didn't stop. Ten minutes later, the doctor had detached the leg from the thigh and tossed it into the pile of limbs. He took a small flap of skin that once belonged to Jackson's now detached leg and folded it over the stub, sealing it with a yellow ointment and finished it with gauzy linen fabric.

"If he wakes up, someone should be with him. He is gonna be in a lot of pain. You gonna stay with him, soldier?"

"Yes, sir!" Nelson said almost cutting off the doctor.

"Good luck." And with that the doctor went to the next bed to diagnose another soldier.

Jackson began to violently shake in his sleep shortly after the doctor moved on to other patients. Nelson took hold of both Jackson's shoulders and pinned them to the cot in an attempt to settle him, as if he thought he could squeeze hard enough to cease the shaking. Jackson's mind was still void of any thought. After a minute, Jackson's convulsions ceased.

I stood there and observed the two of them. Nelson was slumped down into a makeshift chair beside Jackson's cot, arms crossed over his chest willing him to wake up. He jumped at Jackson's slightest movement. After two hours of waiting, Jackson began to cough and his eyes opened slowly. His forehead was slick with cold sweat, even though it was a million degrees outside. Jackson's eyes bounced around the camp, desperate to get his bearings. He began to fight his way out of the bed and rolled what was once two legs over the side of the cot, but only one hit the ground. He fell. As he lifted his face from the dirt, he began to shake at the sight of the stub.

"It still feels like its there, Nels. It feels like I could run across this field." Nelson's face fell. He walked over to Jackson and helped him back into bed, placing a sheet over Jackson's lower body. Jackson's mind was hazy.

"It's just your mind playin' tricks on ya, Jack. You need your rest." Jackson's face was void of color.

"My leg is growing back, Nels. I can feel it growing." Jackson was slipping. Nelson lifted the sheet to look at his leg. It was soaked through with fresh blood.

"Doc! Doc, get over here!" The doctor strolled in a mock run over to Jackson's cot. "Is it normal for him to be losing this much blood?"

The doctor pulled up the sheet to examine the stub. "Nope, not normal at all." The doctor peeled back the dressings and checked the wound, and then his pulse. Blood was spilling down the cot creating a small dark puddle in the dirt. "I'm sorry soldier, but he has already lost too much blood. We tried everything we could." The doctor patted Nelson on the shoulder as he began to walk to his next patient.

Nelson grabbed the stout doctor by the collar pulling him to within an inch of his face. "Try harder!" The doctor's face turned serious.

"There is nothing more we can do for him now!" he said, his voice trembling. "I'm truly sorry, soldier." Nelson released the doctor aggressively.

He looked down at his friend who was white as a sheet. "I failed her Jackson, I failed you. I promised to keep you safe."

"You didn't fail me, Nelson. You're one of the only people who has never failed me." Jackson forced a smile. His breath was labored.

Nelson dropped to his knees, eye level with Jackson. "What can I do?" he asked.

"Keep her safe. Both of them. Tell 'em I love 'em. They're gonna need you." Jackson's head rolled to the side, eyes open and void staring blankly through me, and exhaled.

"Jackson? Jackson!" Nelson took hold of Jackson's shoulders and shook his lifeless body, watching his limbs wobble aimlessly and fall back into the cot. He was gone. Nelson's head fell against the cot, his hand grasping Jackson's. Nelson began to beat the sides of the cot with his fists causing Jackson's lifeless body to jump. He let out a long yell, a yell that came from deep within his chest. He wept for his friend, his brother, his comrade.

A tap on my shoulder startled me. It was Jackson, standing right in front of me. He could see me, touch me. "How? I don't ..."

"Did you find what you were lookin' for?" he said. I stood silent, too shocked to form thoughts or words. "I don't know what you're lookin' for, but whatever it is, learn from it. You're here for a reason. You're here to not make the same mistakes I did."

"How am I seeing you? Aren't you technically me?" I asked confused.

"The soul evolves when it passes to the next life, yet it holds on to your most powerful emotions and aches from your former selves, plaguing the body with its most intense pains and joys. We are all individuals within one soul, operating for one purpose, to learn from each journey and become whole."

"What is my purpose? My journey? What am I suppose to learn from this?"

"That's a loaded question, son. I hope you will let me know the answer when you start siftin' through Pandora's box."

Jackson turned to look back at Nelson. He was removing the locket from Jackson's body, and then gingerly closed Jackson's eyes. I still didn't know what it all meant.

"It means family, above all else," he said. He could hear me. "You protect those you love and set a fine example for 'em, something I failed to do. I thought that fightin' this war would protect them, protect us. I thought it was the right thing to do for my family, but all war is useless. Nothing good comes from murdering your brothers, just pain and death. Half of us didn't even know what we were fightin' for, just that it was our duty as members of the Confederacy to protect our land. They filled our heads with nonsense about slavery ending and that it would devastate the economy, makin' us all destitute. We didn't think beyond that, beyond what had always been normal.

Fighting in this war was the mistake that I made in this life. Not standing up or taking the time to understand what it all meant. I just followed blindly, something you have clearly learned from already, and for that I'm grateful. But I reckon that's not the only lesson you'll take from here. It seems you have a long ride ahead of you. It's been a pleasure, Nathan." With that, he bowed, tipping his hat toward me, and the world went black.

Being in the black was like being lost in space. You have no movement, you have no body, you only have your thoughts, and mine were running wild. It was only for a moment, and then in a snap, I am dropped into a new chaotic universe.

People are running everywhere. I recognized myself immediately though I can only see myself from behind. I am watching him from outside of his body. The way he was standing, the way he swung his arms when he ran was so akin to my body's movements now.

In this life, I have dark curly hair and bronze sun-kissed skin. My past self is holding the hand of a girl with equal features, but slightly fairer skin, pulling her behind aggressively as he runs. She lags behind, tripping over her long white dress. She turns back toward me revealing her face, staring into what she is running from. Her brown eyes are swollen red and horrified. A tiny speck of gold peeks out from her iris. I run to keep up with them, but my feet feel like I'm trudging through quicksand. Just as I turn my head to see what we are running from, I feel a hiccup that radiates throughout my body and I fall, but don't hit the ground. I fall through it. Back into the black.

As quickly as I was thrown into the vision, I'm thrust back out. I open my eyes to reveal the faces of two worried women staring at me. Dr. Rose grabs my wrist and Liv runs her hand through my damp hair. I could feel cold sweat dripping down my forehead. My body feels weak, like I've been working out, but I haven't moved from this couch.

"His vitals are fine. How are you feeling, Mr. James?" Dr. Rose says as she shines a bright light in my eyes. Liv hands me a glass of water and some crackers from the snack table behind me.

"I'm … I don't know." I couldn't articulate how I felt in words. I was still reeling from the last vision. *What is the rest of the story? Do I even want to know?*

Dr. Rose proceeded to tell me I was out for an hour and made "a lot of progress," whatever that means. "I apologize for bringing you out so abruptly. You were starting to display some unusual behavior. You started to speak about a war, and then you went silent for around an hour. You would respond to my questions by tapping me, like a code, but I didn't understand what it meant. I only woke you when you began to shiver uncontrollably."

"What did you see, Nate?" Liv said eager to know more.

"I think he will need to speak with me first. Alone, if that's okay."

Liv was hesitant at first, but then exited when I gave her a reassuring nod. Really, I was starting to freak out. I watched Liv walk slowly to the door and quietly shut it behind her.

"What the hell was that, Doc!?" I said almost spilling water all over the couch. "I mean, did you inception my dreams or some crazy shit like that?" My eyes feel like they are bulging out of my face. The feeling of cold sweat and scorching heat radiates though my body. My heart has not stopped racing since I woke up.

"How are you feeling right now, Mr. James?"

"Seriously? How am I feeling? Like I've just time warped through Middle fucking Earth! How do you think I feel?"

"Calm down, Mr. James, this is all very normal. If you would like me to help you make sense of this, I can, but you need to settle down and speak to me about what you saw. I know it can be scary at first, but once you understand them, it could benefit you in your current journey."

Here she goes again about my "journey." Maybe I'm just a normal guy who does normal things. I'm not supposed to change the world in any spectacular way. I'm just supposed to live, die and then who knows what.

"I was in a war."

"Which war? There have been many wars throughout history. Where did you begin?"

"The Civil War. I was a marksman. A good one too, which is weird because guns from that era were not really accurate, but apparently I was the best in the Confederacy. I was shot in the leg during battle, but didn't die. I had to have my leg amputated and that's what killed me. The doctor didn't even seem surprised or upset. Just like it was a regular day at the office for him. The weird thing is, this all took place in Virginia near where I grew up and I swear I've been there before."

"It is not uncommon to be brought back to places of significance in future lives, especially if that past life was particularly scarring. Think of it as your soul giving you a chance to right past wrongs. Did you see anything else that seemed familiar while you were in this life?" asked Dr. Rose.

"There was one thing that confused me. My best friend was there. It didn't look like him, but I felt like it was him. And Liv was there, too. I only saw a picture, but it was definitely her. How is that possible?"

"Throughout our journeys, we often come back to a physical form with the same souls. You may find that they each play a different part in your existence at different times. Sometimes they may play a larger roll and sometimes they are just acquaintances. It is interesting, however, that you were able to identify them so easily. How were you certain it was them?"

"With Darrin, I just had a feeling by the way we interacted that it was him. As for Liv, that was a bit different. It was in her eyes and mouth, the softness of her face. She has a golden freckle in her eye that appeared in both visions. Just like the one she has now. It's not immediately recognizable, but if you look for it, it's there."

"Interesting," said Dr. Rose as she scribbled in her notebook. She was writing so fast it looked like her hands couldn't keep up with her thoughts. "What do you mean by both versions? Did you have another vision?"

"Wait, what are you writing? I don't want to be some science project."

"Just notes." She said awkwardly hesitant. It was the first time I had seen her uncomfortable throughout this whole ordeal. Even when I was making fun of it she kept her cool. "What was your other vision about?" she asked.

"It kind of felt like this recurring dream I've been having since I met Liv, but a little different. I don't think I finished seeing that life. It felt like I was ripped out of there so fast, and then I was here." *That life? Seriously, Nate, who are you?*

"What does this dream depict?" asked Dr. Rose.

"It's always about me and Liv. We are enjoying a day in a meadow, or on a boat, or watching the sunset on a beach, and then I lose her. Not like she runs away or anything, but she actually slips away. Sometimes she literally turns into sand, sometimes water, sometimes she ignites into a fire that I can't put out or feel the burn on my own skin and she turns to ash. Either way, she literally slips through my fingers. That's the last image I see before I wake up."

"Dreams can represent manifestations of fears from your past lives, especially dreams that you have more than once. It signifies someone trying to guide you. Sometimes, dreams can even depict your past lives. Have you ever had a dream where you see someone you know, but it doesn't look like them? Like how you recognized your best friend and Ms. Hammond in your regression today?"

In fact, I had. More times than I can count. It was always the same person, my father. Since his death, he would randomly show up, sometimes as a passerby on the street, sometimes as a patron in a diner or a bar. He would just sit in the background and watch me, taking on new skin each time. I try to go after him, to catch up with him, but he always disappears before I can reach him.

"Yeah, but what does that have to do with this?"

"Those are people from your past lives that you know in this life. It is a very powerful, deep connection when that happens. Do you record these dreams?"

"What, like in a journal? No."

"I recommend you begin keeping one for the upcoming

week and we'll meet again next week. Would you be open to that?" Dr. Rose asked hesitantly.

I have to admit I was intrigued, but not sold on the whole thing. "Yeah, I would do it again," I promised half-heartedly.

She walked over to her bookcase and pulled out a worn paperback book. "I have never seen someone respond to a regression like you did just now. You completely shut me out, like someone else was in your mind taking you through your lives." She handed me the tattered book. "I think you should take this home with you. It is a book written by a very famous doctor, with a Ph.D. and many other accolades, who stumbled upon a past life regression experience through a patient of his. It's about his skeptical journey through what was happening right in front of his eyes and his eventual belief that our souls inhabit more than one physical form. You may find that Chapter 10 is of particular interest." Dr. Rose walked to the door to leave, but turned at the last moment. "I really do hope I see you back here, Mr. James. I would hate for your message to go unfinished,"

"What message?"

She turned back toward me and pointed to the book. "Read."

During the cab ride home, Liv was oddly quiet, trying to process everything that had happened. She opened her mouth to speak and then stopped herself, staring out the window.

"It's just so weird," she said, finally. "I mean, it makes a lot of sense, the Civil War thing. I have always been fascinated by that era. I have so many questions I didn't think to ask before."

My heart jumped into my throat remembering my vision. I decided not to mention to Liv that I was the dead man who abandoned her. I just smiled and kissed her hand.

When she is quiet like this, I don't want to interrupt her. It's the look she gets when her mind is working brilliance. You can tell something beautiful is going on in there. She's had that look less and less these days. It's nice to see it again.

By the time we got home, Liv was a little more talkative. I told her a few things about Jackson and being a soldier, but conveniently left out the part where she was the woman I left behind.

"How weird is it that we lived in the same time together! Do you think we knew each other?" She was reaching. She knew I was holding something back from her.

"Maybe. It was a much smaller world back then," I said, passively evading her question.

"I wonder who the man was, in my past life. I wish I could have seen them like you did. I'm thinking I might go back, to do what you did. What do you think?"

I wanted to get up and scream, "NO! That stuff was insane!" but that would just make her want to do it more. She was rebellious in that way. If we were at a restaurant and the waiter said, "Don't touch this plate, it's hot," she would touch it anyway, just to confirm it for herself, even if she did end up getting burned.

"If you think you need to go back, I think you should," I said, in hopes it would be lackluster enough for her to forget about it.

"Is that Nathan James coming down off his high horse about believing in something that can't be explained? I don't believe it!" Liv said sarcastically.

"Well, I can't explain what I saw, but it definitely felt pretty real. I don't know if I'm off my high horse, but my foot is definitely out of the stirrup."

After Liv went to bed that evening, I was feeling a little sauced from my celebratory scotch. With some liquid courage, I decided to take a dive into that book. The title read *Past Lives: Surprising an Analytical Mind*, by Dr. Ryan White. The cover was well worn, like it had been read a thousand times. A mess of notes and highlighted sections littered the pages without disrupting the text. I skimmed the first two chapters, but ended up skipping ahead to my recommended reading: chapter 10, "The Dream Chapter".

There are many types of dreams. Dreams can bring to light souls you connected with or events that happened in a past life. You will often see people you know in your current life, but they look different or do things than they normally wouldn't do. Sometimes, you will see that person as they are now, but in the context of an event that happened in the past. For example, if someone close to you died tragically in the past, your soul manifests that fear that it could happen again and the guilt that you couldn't stop it, resulting in nightmarish dreams about your loved one dying in the present in a similar manner.

Dreams can also provide guidance from lost loved ones. They will appear in our dreams to send us a message or as a sign of comfort. Sometimes they look like themselves, as you knew them, sometimes in the form of a past life. This symbolizes a strong spiritual guide looking to connect.

I felt goosebumps crawl up my arms and legs. I was haunted by those nightmares about Liv, but the dreams with my father were different. I haven't ever admitted this before, but I always thought he was trying to tell me something. It sounds insane, so I just pushed it to the corners of my mind and called it coincidence, but what if it's not? After today, I don't know what's up from down. I feel more lost now than I felt before all of this. I have to go back. I have to know more.

Three scotches in, I decided it would be a brilliant idea to call Dr. Rose's office. It was almost 1 a.m., so I figured I would just leave a message, but to my surprise, she picked up.

"Hello?"

"Dr. Rose?" I said, slightly slurring.

"Yes?"

"Doc, it's Nate. Uh, Nathan James?" I stammered over my words like I was talking to my mom after a wild field party in high school.

"Ah yes, Mr. James. What can I do for you?"

"I want to do another regression."

"Alright. Will Ms. Hammond be accompanying you?"

"No, just me this time. And I would appreciate it if this was not mentioned to her. I don't want her to know about what I saw."

"Very well, Mr. James. All of my patient files are confidential, I assure you."

"Will 2 p.m. next Sunday work? Liv will be at her restaurant job, so I can slip away."

"Yes, that works fine for me." She paused a moment, like she was scribbling something. "Oh, and please remember a cup of coffee tomorrow morning. Alcohol makes the mind grow weary. Goodnight, Mr. James." And with that, she hung up the phone. That night, I drifted to sleep as soon as my head hit the pillow.

I'm standing on a bustling street surrounded by unfamiliar faces. People buzz around like I'm invisible. In the distance, a man in a fedora stands still amongst the commotion. His head is tilted downward obscuring his eyes. *I know this game. I know who you are.* I push through the crowd toward the man. As if on cue, he turns and walks away from me. The crowd parts to let him through and moves into my path, blocking me from getting to him. "Dad!" I yell finally. The man stops, but the passersby continue to shuffle. "Dad, wait for me!" I run toward him, knocking into every person in my way. Just before I could reach my hand to touch him, he vanishes into the crowd.

My eyes open slowly to reveal the ceiling of my bedroom. The clock reads 2:36 a.m. I am so groggy I can barely place my surroundings. I turn to my nightstand and dig out my small sketchbook I keep by the bed in case I wake up with an idea. "Fedora. Crowd. Dad. Running. Call name. Gone," I scribble in near illegible script before succumbing to the sleep.

CHAPTER EIGHT

Monday Morning, 8 a.m.

Monday, again. My alarm clock beeped five times before I allowed it to wake me. I poured myself into the shower, preparing for yet another day of passionless misery. Don't get me wrong, my job isn't that bad. The people are cool and the job itself is pretty easy, but every day it takes me further and further away from the reason I moved to New York in the first place. The money is the only thing that keeps me going. It isn't great, but it pays the bills.

As the hot water flows down my back, I can smell last night's scotch wash away. I still couldn't shake yesterday's adventure. Jackson, the incomplete life I saw, my inexplicable dreams. I think Dr. Rose knows more than she's letting on.

The subway was packed with the usual Monday latecomers. I squished myself between a man in a $3,000 suit and a construction worker in a neon vest just to fit in the car. I nearly nailed the rich guy with my coffee when the doors closed, soliciting a "how dare you exist in my presence" look. The subway is the only place in the world where you can feel alone and claustrophobic at the same time. Everyone is inside their own world, dominated by headphones and tablets. No one else exists outside of the noises singing in their heads.

I arrived at my usual 23rd Street stop and fought my way up the crowded staircase, almost pile driving an old lady in the process. That might sound bad, but this is New York and if you're slow, you get run over no matter who you are. I'm my usual 10 minutes late, but so is everyone else. The office is nearly empty save for a few overeager employees looking for a promotion. I just don't care that much.

Mulling over my morning coffee, I start surfing the Internet for new gallery openings when my boss messages me.

JAN: Let's meet in the conference room in 5?

NATHAN: No problem. See you in 5.

It is way too early for a meeting and my boss is actually in the office for once. This isn't good. I immediately erase my search history and begin working on the endless Excel sheet of names, addresses and phone numbers I had been compiling since I started here a year ago. Crap, what if they saw my history? *I'm allowed to look at other things at work, they even said so! Shit.*

After the longest five minutes of my life, I met Jan in the conference room, but she isn't alone. The CEO was sitting across from her, fiddling with his phone, disconnected from his employees and seemingly the world. I sit down beside Jan with a notebook; ready to capture any useless wisdom she might spout this morning.

"Nathan, we called you in here because we are seeing a decrease in sales in our department. No one seems to be bringing in a lot of business, especially you." I feel an unprecedented heat begin to spread through my neck and into my face. "Nathan, we are going to begin downsizing the department and unfortunately we can't afford to keep you on board with us."

My mind was wild. All I could see are big red dollar signs piling up, one on top of the other. I was too shocked to speak or even react. My blank expression must reflect my internal monologue because Jan began her spiel about how much she values me, giving the old "it's not you, it's me" excuse. I was too in shock to focus on the details of my firing. When I finally gathered my thoughts enough to speak, "Thank you for the opportunity," was all I could muster.

The CEO, finally looking up from his iPhone, said, "No problem, Ned. We wish you the best of luck in your future endeavors." What a guy.

The walk back to my desk was in slow motion. I looked around at my co-workers, blissfully unaware of what had just occurred. My chest started to tighten, like I couldn't breathe. I sat down at my desk and mindlessly packed up a year of my life. I looked around at my colleagues, my friends, but was too embarrassed to even say goodbye. I will see some of them again, but most were just people I saw every day out of circumstance. As I made my way toward the door, no one looks up to question why I'm leaving so early in the day. They were probably thinking, "Oh, Nate is going to get yet another coffee. That caffeine junky!" not, "Oh shit, Nate just got canned."

As I make my way to the large double glass doors leading to the elevators, Jan stops me.

"I'm sorry this didn't work out, Nate. You're a good guy

and a great worker, but the company is in flux right now. I wish things were different." I nodded my head respectfully, thanked her again for the opportunity and waited for the elevator to hit the 6th floor.

During the ride down, I couldn't seem to feel sad. By all standards of bad things happening, this should rate pretty high up there, but I just couldn't seem to give this event the freak-out moment it deserved. I felt relief. How could I possibly feel relieved? Money is going to be tight, maybe I will have to move out of New York, and all I felt is relieved?

When I hit the sidewalk I pulled out my phone to call Liv, but hesitated. How am I going to tell her I'm jobless? I had never felt like this before. I was so ashamed.

"Hey babe! How's work?"

"Liv I gotta tell you something, but don't freak."

"Oh my gosh, what happened?!"

"I got fired today. Well, let go. The department is downsizing and they are making cuts and I guess I was one of them. I'm so sorry, Liv. I will look for a job right away and get back on my feet. They are paying me a two-week severance so we should be fine for rent this month and it will give me some time to find something else." I was talking so fast I was beginning to stumble over my words.

"Babe, everything is going to be okay," she said, calmly interrupting my banter. "We will work it out. You can get unemployment for a while and we can cut back on frivolous expenses. I can pick up a couple more shifts at the restaurant for extra money and we will be golden. Stop worrying and go home. I will fix dinner tonight and we can hash it out over copious amounts of wine, and the best part is you don't have to worry about waking up tomorrow morning to a hangover and having to go to work!" Liv had a knack for turning a negative into a positive.

"Are you sure you're okay with this? I mean, you have a stay-at-home boyfriend now."

"I find that oddly arousing, actually," she said with a chuckle. "I'll see you at home when I get out of work. Try to get out of your own head for a minute. Why don't you go over to the Met and chill for a little bit. It's a beautiful day. I can meet you on the roof for a drink after work if you want? My treat?"

"Okay, meet you there."

"Jobs come and go, they aren't what is really important. I love you and we have each other. Remember that."

"Love you, too. See you later."

I meandered blindly around Manhattan until I found myself at the base of the famous Metropolitan Museum of Art staring up the giant staircase to the entrance. The steps were void of their usual crowd due to the fact it was noon on a workday. Inside, I paid my usual $1 for entry instead of the "suggested donation" of $25, but felt slightly better about it due to my recent job loss. I headed over to my favorite wing, the Egyptian exhibit. The Met had built an entire wing just to house this small Egyptian temple in the arms of New York. It's truly a spectacular sight, no matter how many times you've seen it. Light poured into the windowed wing where the Temple of Dendur stood. Usually this part of the Metropolitan is bustling with tourists snapping photos and posing in front of the temple's iconic entrance, but today the wing was silent. I found a seat on the edge of the fountain encircling the exhibit, just close enough to examine the temple. The small moat was alive with the glitter of various coins thrown in by tourists visiting from every corner of the world.

In an attempt to escape my morning, I allowed my mind to wander through the maze of etchings covering the ancient temple. Some of them were clearly hieroglyphics, but what people don't always see is the graffiti. Not like graffiti you typically see spraypainted on old buildings or subway cars. These are etchings that extend back for generations from invaders, visitors, even locals. It is amazing to think that something can stay around that long, touch so many generations of great people, and now it just sits stagnant in front of a loser like me, looking to it for answers it can't provide. The longer I sat, the more depressed I became. The person who created this temple achieved something I covet. He created something that stood the test of time. He carved his name, literally, on the face of history. I will never be able to do something like that.

Before I knew it, I had been sitting in the same spot for close to 3 hours. Not a moment too soon, my phone buzzes with a text:

LIV: Got cut from work early. Want me to meet you at the Met now?

NATE: Nah. The Met is just depressing me. It's reminding me of what a loser I am. Meet at Biddy's?

LIV: OH! So it's THAT kind of drunken pity party. Okay, meet you there. I will call Darrin, too.

LIV: You're not a loser. The Met will be coming to you one day.

* * *

My head is pounding. I feel like my arms and legs are permanently pinned to my mattress. My unquenchable thirst is the only thing that woke me from my beer-induced coma.

"Heeeey buddy," Liv said in a soft voice, like she was talking to a child.

"Water. Please. Dying."

"I got it for you right on the bedside table with 2 aspirin. Do you want some coffee to accompany that hangover?"

"Please. Coffee. Yes. Dying."

"Okay buddy. Want me to go get a bacon, egg and cheese for you?"

"Please. Yes. Bacon. Lots."

"Okay, be right back." Liv grabbed her purse and headed out the door to the bodega. Instinctively, I curl to her side of the bed and cocoon myself in the covers. I want to reach for the water on the bedside, but water is so heavy when it's in a glass. If only it would float to me.

A few minutes later, I hear the front door shut gently and the comforting smell of coffee and bacon hits my nostrils. I feel my stomach start to rumble and not in a comforting way. A moment later, I was hugging the porcelain goddess for dear life.

After an hour of puking my guts up, I called Darrin to see how he was doing. Like most normal employed people, he was at work suffering with his hangover.

"Dude, I have already thrown up three times in the work bathroom. This is literally the worst hangover of my life. I am totally hating you right now," Darrin said referring to my lack of employment.

"D, I barely remember anything after leaving the bar." I hear Darrin let out an unusually enthusiastic chuckle for his current state. "What's so funny?"

"Nate, I literally carried you home in my arms like a small broken child last night. Did Liv not show you the pictures? It was hilarious and really sad at the same time. You kept saying 'D, you're my hero'. I can't believe you don't remember!"

Slowly the blurry memories of last night began to filter their way back into my brain. Three rounds of shots, followed by countless beers, followed by free pity shots from the bartender. The inevitable drunk guilt that lies in wait at the bottom of every hangover has reared its ugly head.

"Man, I'm sorry. Was I really that bad?" I asked hesitantly.

"I mean yeah, but understandably so. For a guy that just got fired, you were actually really happy last night."

"Well, thanks for taking care of me, bro. I'm sorry I was such a mess," I said, hoping for forgiveness.

"Man, don't worry about it. You would have done the same for me."

"Yeah, except the carrying part," I said, laughing for the first time that day.

"Alright, I'm back to work. Call you when I'm out."

"Later, D."

Well, at least I wasn't the only one welcoming death with open arms this morning.

CHAPTER NINE

Unemployed

"Babe? I'm heading to work." Liv walked over and gave me a peck on the lips, briefly distracting me from my Netflix trance. "Don't forget, we are going to the Met roof for a drink tonight to see the Jeff Koons exhibit."

"Yup, got it. Are Darrin and Ray coming?"

"No idea. Gotta run! Love you!"

Sunday rolls around so slowly when you're jobless. The first jobless day was okay. I spent most of my time looking for new jobs, trolling every employment site I could find, getting excited at every prospect, and then realizing that over 400 people had applied for the same job. Back down again. The second day, I watched an entire show on Netflix … it was three seasons long. The third day, I slept until 3 p.m., because why wake up? By the fourth day, I was going stir crazy, so I cleaned the entire house, even bleached our ancient bathtub. God knows how many asses that thing has seen over the years. On the fifth day, Liv and I walked in the park, got coffees and just sat in the grass watching the sky. That was the highlight of my week, and yes I am fully aware of how sad that sounds.

Today is the sixth day, my date with Dr. Rose. I have to admit, I am oddly looking forward to it. This whole week I have felt nothing but lost. Even if this stuff isn't real, maybe I will still get some good ideas out of it.

I showed up to Dr. Rose's office looking slightly homeless in my ripped jeans, army coat and beat up Converse sneakers. My joblessness has taken a toll on my desire to look presentable. Thankfully, her receptionist Shelly didn't judge my scruffy appearance and escorted me right into Dr. Rose's office.

"Good afternoon, Mr. James. Please take a seat. Can I get you some coffee?"

"No thank you, I have already had a few cups."

"Very good. Did you have some time to look through the book I loaned you?"

"Yeah, way to warn me."

"I wanted you to discover the similarities for yourself. Did you find anything of particular interest?" she said, almost too knowingly.

"Yes, but you knew that already didn't you?" Dr. Rose gave me a knowing smirk and returned her eyes to her note taking.

"Prior to your regression, I would like to learn a little more about you. Your beliefs, your absolutes, your fears."

"I'm not really religious," I answered quickly, hoping to skirt the subject.

"You aren't religious, yet you wear the medallion of St. Christopher around your neck."

How did she even see that? I kept it hidden for a reason.

"Well, my dad gave it to me. It's not for a religious purpose though; it's just as a symbol. How did you know I wore one? I never keep it outside of my shirt?"

"When did your father pass, Mr. James?" she said, evading my question.

"How did you know that he passed?"

"I'm sure you mentioned it before," she said uncomfortably. "When did he pass?"

I remember the day my father died like it was yesterday. It wasn't some dramatic ousting of life. He just died, plain and simple. His body surrendered to the cancer in his brain and it shut down.

It was June 3. A day I have to live through every year like something life altering didn't occur that warped me for the rest of my life. I remember the coldness of his skin at 2:36 a.m. when my mother brought me to see him one last time. I remember how hard her face looked, like she had fought emotion for so long and there was just nothing left. I remember the funeral home packed with what seemed like a thousand people and the small urn of ash on the altar that we were all there to see. I remember the pungent smell of lilies that hung in the air and the constant reminder of death that accompanied it. I remember my mother and me in the front pew, empty of expression, too overwhelmed to fully grip the reality of the scene around us. I remember Darrin crying silently beside me and his face when he looked at me, willing me to cry with him.

My dad had given Darrin his first beer, taught him how to play the harmonica, given him girl advice, and attended every game he could until he got too sick to climb the bleachers, rooting him on like he was his own. Sometimes I would come home from my afterschool job to find

Darrin and my dad watching TV, just shootin' the breeze. It never bothered me that they were so close – I guess because Darrin was the closest thing to a sibling I ever had. Darrin's parents were divorced and his dad was always out of town, doing something or another for work, or play … who really knew.

My dad was so proud of Darrin when he got his football scholarship, and me when I got into NYU. We both found out just before he got really sick. He took us out to a really fancy dinner to celebrate. "Boys only!" he said, shooting my mom a playful look, "No chicks allowed!" At dinner, he gave us each a small box. I can still hear him saying, "I don't care how old you are, you are always going to need this." Inside the box was the St. Christopher medal on a simple white gold chain.

"Mr. J, when did we become a couple of chicks that you can just buy off with jewelry?" Darrin poked playfully. It was an odd gift for him to give us. Neither of my parents was particularly religious.

"Very funny, Darrin," my father said. "Both of you boys are leaving me. Here, I can keep an eye on you. There, I don't know what kind of hell you're raisin'... and I do expect there to be hell raisin'. St. Christopher is the patron saint of protection, and while I am not a religious man, I think you boys need something to remind yourselves that you aren't invisible. This should remind you to take care of each other, even after I'm gone."

"Dad, don't talk like that. You're not goin' anywhere."

"Son, I am. Whether it's today, tomorrow, ten, twenty years from now, I will be goin' and that's okay. It is the natural order of things. Parents die, kids carry on, and it keeps goin' just like that. Let's not dwell on that though.

Today is not about me. Today is about how proud I am of my boys. Now order anything you want, except the lobster stuffed with Kobe beef. I'm not a Rockefeller." That night, we all ordered the lobster Kobe and enjoyed every last bite.

"He passed right before I went to college," I told Dr. Rose. "I don't really like to talk about it. Can we just go ahead and do the thing again?"

"Of course," she said begrudgingly, "though I do have one request. During our last session you shut me out completely, which I don't believe was intentional. I believe that I was shut out for a purpose, so that you could see your lives completely uninhibited by the outside world. You may not believe this, but I think the master spirits wanted to entice you into accepting them. It seems that they have plans for you. Whether you believe this or not, I ask that you open your heart and your mind to the idea. If this is just a fun story to tell your buddies, I think that this is not the time for you. If you are truly looking for betterment in your life, then take this experience and use it to your advantage."

I was a little taken back by the doc. She was almost scolding me. "Okay. I'm a skeptic, but you have to understand, I grew up in a town of Bible-beating followers, blindly accepting what their parents believe, because it's what their parents' parents believed. My parents raised me to be a free thinker, maybe a little too much I guess. I never really felt the need to decide on what I believed in or even if I believed in anything at all. Rebellion against anything supernatural is kind of what I do … or did … but after last week, well all I'm trying to say is I wouldn't be here if I wasn't intrigued."

Dr. Rose cracked a small smile. "Good. Then this time I will lead you through your regression. You will hear me prompt you with questions which you will answer out loud, whether you know it or not."

"Whatever you say, Doc! Let's do this."

The relaxation process took less time than I expected. I fell right into it like an old habit. Maybe after the week I've had, this is what I needed. It felt so good to just feel nothing, to let go of everything weighing me down. I followed my childhood path into the black again.

CHAPTER TEN
Faroe Islands, 802 A.D.

"Tell me where you are, Nathan," Dr. Rose requests in her usual low, monotone voice.

We are under attack. There is fire everywhere. I am looking out from a higher point through his eyes, a balcony maybe. The fight has not yet reached to where I am, but I can see it moving my way. I see lots of blood. People are being slaughtered, innocent people. They are my people.

"Tell me what you look like, what you are wearing."

I am dressed in a tunic like top that hangs over a pair of thick pants tucked into leather boots. My torso is layered with a leather vest and chainmail. I feel powerful, like a warrior. It's warm all around me, but a cold breeze sweeps through, cutting the heat like a knife. I feel the pull of a sword hanging from my belt on my left side.

The light is dim. To my right is a large bed with a canopy. All of the objects in the room are very feminine and opulent. I catch my reflection in a silver pitcher on the vanity. My hair is light brown and slightly curly. My skin looks dark and weathered, but I am young and muscular, around 22 years old. I am speckled with scars on my hands and arms. My jaw is sharp, making my face look hard. My eyes are wide and brown, but they don't retain the same harshness. They stare back at me softly, almost worried.

"Can you describe your surroundings? Is there anyone else with you?"

I feel a hand grasp mine from behind, interrupting my thoughts of the blood bath outside. I hadn't noticed anyone else in the room with me. The hand belongs to a tall woman, similar in age, with long wavy blonde hair. She is slender with very blue eyes. She wears a thin white dress, almost like a nightgown, covered by a deep blue robe clasped in the front with a jeweled broach. Her head is adorned with a silver headpiece that comes to a downward point and grazes the top her forehead. The etchings inside the headpiece are intricate and clearly hand carved by a valued metal worker. Not quite a crown, but something of value. When she touches me, I feel softer, lighter. I love her so much it is overwhelming, almost unexplainable. I realize his worries do not lie with the people outside this window – they lie with her.

"Do you recognize this woman?"

I search her eyes for some recognition, though it's hardly necessary. I feel the same way in my present life as I did in my past. It's her again. Every time, it's always her. Unfortunately, I have a vague idea about how this will end. Just like the others. Losing her all over again.

She doesn't look much different than she does now. This version of Liv is slightly more muscular and broad, but her features are very similar. I feel the faint tremble of her hand in mine as she peers over the balcony into the scene below. He tightens his grasp in response.

"Brandt, we have to go. They are moments from infiltrating the castle," the woman says to me. Her voice is steady and low. It takes me a moment to realize she is speaking a foreign language, Swedish, I think? But it registers to me as English. Her eyes are steely and serious, locked on mine. She holds a long sword dotted with deep red stones on the handle in her right hand.

"We must find my father and get him to safety. They are pushing through the front gate, but have not yet crossed the bridge. Our army is holding them off, but it is only a matter of time until they rush through the castle doors. If we hurry, we can escape through the hidden tunnel in my father's quarters," she says pulling him toward the door. Her father must be the king.

I notice a modest ring on the third finger of her left hand. Compared to the opulence of her sword, it seems to pale in comparison. He rubs it with his thumb, stroking her hand. She looks down, and then glances up at him with a smile that spreads through her eyes.

"Soon, my love. He will approve. Ease your worries," she said. She stretches up to kiss him softly. He brings her into him with both arms and swallows her with his embrace. Though she is tall and broad in stature, she seems almost tiny in Brandt's embrace. He trembles as she deepens her kiss into him. Both of her feet are dangling above the floor as she pushes herself into his strong embrace. She tries to pull away, but he fights it, pulling her closer just a moment longer before putting her down. Brandt puts both hands into her hair, cradling her head.

"Today, Elisabeth. We must tell him today. I'm not sure how much longer I can pretend."

She nods her head. "Today then," she said pulling him toward the door. An arrow strikes the door in front of us, flying in from the open window. We duck to the ground, moving toward the door as one succinct unit.

It's clear he is a soldier and not fit for her – his dress, his calloused hands, all evidence of Brandt's place in this time. She doesn't seem to notice. Her hand is steady in his, like it has been there a thousand times before.

"Explain the scene. What is happening around you?"

She pulls me through double doors of her bedroom into a long hallway. Her footsteps are calculated and swift like his. Left, right, left, right, carefully placing each movement, floating like a ghost throughout the hallow castle. His eyes dart around the hallway and catch a sliver of movement to our right. A man dressed in armor is coming toward us with his sword raised. Before Brant can turn to face the intruder, Elisabeth raises her sword reflexively. She strikes at a glimmer of pale skin between the intruder's helmet and chest piece, expertly slicing it with her sword. The man falls to his knees, blood pouring from his wound. A spray of blood stains her white dress, but she doesn't seem fazed. Her stance is flawless. She is swift and direct, like a warrior.

"I'm impressed, Elisabeth," he says.

"I had a very attentive instructor," she said shooting him a sly look. I see a fragment of Liv in Elisabeth's sarcasm. I hear a noise from behind me and before my mind can process the source, Brandt has ended the man behind him in the same manner.

Elisabeth motions silently for Brandt to follow her.

Another man appears ahead of her, his sword inches away from her throat. She drops to her knees evading his sword and strikes at the intruder's ankles, slicing his Achilles tendon. A murderous scream escapes him as he drops to the floor. She rises in one graceful motion, mercifully cutting the man's throat, ending his unrelenting screams.

I feel a smile spread across Brandt's face. He feels prideful, because Elisabeth killed a man, but for giving her the ability to protect herself. Another man comes running down the hall. His clothing is different from the others, similar to mine. Elisabeth and Brandt hold their swords at their sides as he approaches.

"Your Majesty," the man says bowing. "Your father has requested I come for you, though it looks as though you have already been retrieved," the man says giving Brandt a devious look. *He knows.* Brandt's mind starts to panic, though I cannot feel a trace of it on his face.

"I was down the hall from Eliza … her majesty's quarters when I heard the fighting begin. I immediately ran to her aid."

"He was very helpful, James," Elisabeth said coldly.

"Apparently not helpful enough," James said, motioning to the traces of blood on Elisabeth's clothes.

"Do you recognize this man James?" I hear Dr. Rose ask from what feels like a million miles away.

He looks familiar. I don't think I like him in my current life. I think he's Billy Reid.

"Please take me to my father, James." Elisabeth's voice is cutting. I would not want to be on the receiving end of that.

We follow James down a long hallway that turned abruptly into a short corridor. At the end, there are two large doors adorned with colorful engravings and glass tiles. These must be the King's quarters.

Elisabeth doesn't knock, but instead swings open the two doors together, with Brandt and James following her. The King is sitting on the windowsill, unarmed, in nightclothes similar to Elisabeth's. His hair is long and ashy blond, accented by an impressive beard. As he turns to direct his attention toward us, I feel Brandt immediately drop to one knee with his head down before making eye contact. Elisabeth stands straight, though she knows she is supposed to bow. Brandt fights a smirk. She's stubborn, just like Liv. *Good to know some things never change.*

As Brandt lifts his head, he meets the terrified gaze of the King. Out of the corner of his eye, I see a white-faced James scurry out of the room as fast as he can. In a split second, I am forced out of Brandt, now watching him from the corner of the room. He turns to see five guards coming toward Elisabeth and the King. Elisabeth raises her sword to the first man, severing his arm from his body in one swift motion. Brandt snaps into a soldier, fighting alongside Elisabeth like a choreographed dance. Brandt and Elisabeth work systematically through the line of soldiers. The King watches the two, confused. His brow wrinkles in such a familiar way. My father. The King is my father.

Elisabeth's sword locks with a soldier trying to strike her from overhead. She is holding him off, but the sword is slowly inching toward her throat. Instinctively, she places her foot on his stomach, pushing him away just long enough to unlock their swords. Brandt lunges at the man, planting his sword behind the soldier's knees, slicing into his muscle. I count four bodies on the floor and immediately turn around. The King is being held with a sword at his throat. Elisabeth's face hardens.

"Drop your weapons," the man says calmly. Brandt slowly obeys, his eyes not leaving the intruder's. Though I'm not in his body, I can feel his heart pounding against my chest. His mind is wild, scared almost. Elisabeth slowly begins to obey the intruder's command as well. Just as her sword is placed on the stone floor, her hand moves to her ankle and she quickly removes a small knife and expertly throws it into the intruder's upper thigh. The man screams, but he never drops his grasp on the King. Elisabeth reaches for her sword, but before she can lift it, the intruder draws the blade across the King's jugular in one swift motion, blood pouring onto his white nightclothing.

Reflexively, Elisabeth stabs the man through the belly, twisting the blade. She stares directly into his eyes as if she can't miss the life leaving them.

Brandt rushes to catch the King as he falls. His eyes are wide and terrified, his left hand pressed against the Kings neck attempting to stop the blood flow from the gaping wound in the King's neck. I feel my stomach drop. I don't know if I can watch my father die a second time, even if he is someone else.

Brandt's mind flashes to a memory from his childhood. A 5-year-old Brandt is chasing a small Elisabeth through the halls of the castle when he runs face first into the King's leg, falling back onto his rear. A long stern look spreads across the King's face. Every inch of Brandt is stiff as a board with fear. The King just smiles and pats his head. "My boy, don't hurt yourself. Your mother will likely kill me if I deliver her boy back with scrapes and bruises."

The memory spreads through Brandt like the first sip of warm tea.

Elisabeth rushes to her father's side. The King's eyes flutter, fighting to stay open. He looks from Brandt to Elisabeth grasping their hands with what little force he had left and thrusts them together, holding them tightly in place. He looked up at Brandt with a faint smile just before the light left his eyes. Elisabeth was silent. There were no tears, no screams of terror, nothing. She just sat there, motionless. Her blue eyes locked on his, like she reverted inside herself to hide.

A loud crash comes from the hall outside the King's chambers. Brandt grabs his sword and forces Elisabeth over his shoulder. She is silent as he carries her to a small hidden door beneath the tapestry. He forces the door inward revealing a long passageway. Brandt presses the door shut behind him, careful not to leave any trace of them for the intruders to follow. The passageway is pitch black, but Brandt seems to have no trouble navigating it. I follow the faint sound of his footsteps around a corner and into a circular room.

I hear Brandt feel along the wall for something. A spark of light appears as he places a torch in the sconce on the wall. He gently places Elisabeth on the ground, her hair illuminated by the firelight. She stares straight ahead, as if in a trance. Her blue eyes, once electric, look gray and pale. Brandt slowly sits on the floor next to her, not looking away from her for a moment. Hesitantly he raises his hand to pull back the hair from her eyes. Elisabeth flinches backward at first, but then gives in to his embrace.

"Elisabeth," he whispers, "when my father died …"

"Brandt, don't. You didn't watch your father murdered

because of your actions."

"Yes, I did." Elisabeth shifts her gaze to meet his. "When my father died, he left my mother with little money; we were quite poor even when he was alive and working. She had never worked outside of our home or left me alone to find work in the village because I was so young. My mother didn't ask him for help, but your father gave it to her anyway. Why he chose to help us, I will never know. We had no money, no stature. He had nothing to gain. It is what I admired most about him. Your father gave us a chance to better our lives. He taught me like a father would a son. He helped me grow into the man that I am now." Elisabeth's face was softening with every word as she listened to a rare, unknown tale of her father. "Today, the only father I knew died in my arms and I could do nothing to help him."

Elisabeth inched toward Brandt until she was leaning into his chest. "Why didn't you ever tell me that?" she asked.

"It is something I've never discussed with anyone." Though the darkness, I see a small smile break onto Elisabeth's face.

"Take yourself to the next big event in this lifetime. What do you see?"

The scene is changing. In a blink, I am outside standing at the edge of a body of water. I am looking on to the scene as it unfolds, independent of Brandt's body. On the shore just inches from the tide, there is a small boat adorned with various engravings holding the body of the King draped in a long fur, probably the result of a hunt. The inside of the boat is lined with hay. Brandt hangs his head in the front row of mourners gathered behind the

King's pyre. Elisabeth stands at the head of the crowd cloaked a long fur cape and large crown, a Queen's crown. Her face is expressionless as she motions to her squire to push the boat into the water. She turns to a man at her left and accepts a bow and flaming arrow from him, aiming it at the boat. She draws the arrow back, its feathers lightly gazing her cheek, and releases it, striking the boat, flames consuming it within seconds. As the boat begins to drift farther and farther down river, Elisabeth drops to one knee bowing her head in respect. Brandt follows, as do the rest of the mourners.

After a moment, Elisabeth rises and faces the crowd.

"Countrymen. We suffer a grave loss today, but it will not be in vain. We will regain the respect of this land. I will lead the charge on our enemy tomorrow morning at dawn." A few laughs spilled out amongst the crowd. Elisabeth catches one in the corner of her eye. "Is this laughable to you, James?"

"Well yes, your majesty. A woman leading us into battle is absurd, with all due respect."

As quickly as the words left his lips, Elisabeth lifts a small dagger from inside her fur cape and plants it against James's cheek, cutting deep into his skin from his temple to the corner of his mouth. James suppresses a scream. Elisabeth's face is empty. "You scurried away like a rat when they came for my father. His life depended on your service to this kingdom and you failed him, and now you mock your Queen? The leader of the kingdom you have sworn before God to protect? You are a disgrace to our kingdom, you are a disgrace to the great legacy my father has left behind, but worst of all, you are a disgrace to the countrymen you failed. By order of the Queen, you are now exiled from this kingdom. Let this brand across your face reflect your cowardice to every new home you seek." Her words silenced the small laughs of the crowd until nothing but the lapping of river water could be heard.

"I will lead this charge," Elisabeth says, turning her attention to the crowd, "as I am now the leader of this kingdom. Anyone who agrees with James, may stay behind and allow our kingdom to fall to ruin, to watch your family, your friends, your neighbors be killed by our enemy. If you have respect for my father and this land he made your home, you will fight beside me." A heavy silence fills the air as James weaves his way through the mass of people, his hand grasping his face.

"I will fight with you," Brandt says standing beside her. Murmurs fill the quiet air. It is clear from Brandt's presence at the head of the crowd that he is well-known and respected amongst the people of this kingdom. He is their champion within the castle walls.

In the distance, I see a man make his way through the crowd until he is face-to-face with Brandt. He is a short, rugged-looking man. He looks slightly older, but that could be due to circumstance. He extends his hand to Brandt. "I will fight with you, brother."

"Thank you, Aleksander." As Brandt reaches to shake Aleksander's hand, it becomes clear that the man is Darrin, following me into battle once again. I don't feel as though he and Brandt know each other well, but Brandt trusts him. The crowd follows Aleksander's lead.

"We will fight with you, your Majesty."

"We will as well!"

A quiet smile crosses her lips, but doesn't reach her eyes. "At dawn we will reclaim what is ours!" Shouts of agreement fill the air.

Elisabeth turns to Brandt and whispers something. The crowd parts through the middle as she walks toward the castle, the townspeople kneeling as she recesses.

"Follow Elisabeth. Where is she going?"

I blink and the scene changes. My eyes open and I am back inside Brandt's mind, viewing the moment though him. He stands facing Elisabeth in a small room. She is clothed in a simple white gown that reached the floor adorned with intricate stitching. The elegant sleeves come to a point that just barely grazes the start of her long fingers. Her shoulders were covered by a red velvet cape lined in brown fur that clasped at her chest with an intricate gold brooch. Her hair is pinned behind her head in a mass of blond braids. A man stands in front of them speaking loudly using dramatic gestures. Brandt does not even acknowledge him. All he can think about is her. Her eyes are staring into him like she can see everything he has ever thought. For just a moment, her face was not stone, but the soft smile he has ingrained in his memory.

When instructed, Brandt places the modest ring on her finger. Then Elisabeth places a gold ring with intricate engravings on Brandt's finger. Brandt looks at her with confusion.

"It was my father's. He would want you to wear it," she said warmly.

I feel a smile spread across his face. Brandt envelops her in his arms and slowly brings her face to his. I feel a familiar tremor run through Brandt's body. He closes his eyes and presses his forehead to hers.

"If you could both kneel, your majesties," says the man. Brandt remains standing until Elisabeth tugs lightly at his left hand as she begins to kneel. He follows uncomfortably. The priest places a large, bejeweled crown on Elisabeth's head and an equally opulent crown on Brandt's.

"I present Queen Elisabeth and King Brandt of the Faroe Islands."

As we turn, we are greeted with three happy faces. *That's weird. I thought this would be kind of a big deal for them.* An older woman stands, her face tear-stained and smiling. She nods in Brandt's direction, clapping. She is so familiar. She runs up to Brandt and wraps her arms around him, squeezing him impressively hard for such a small woman, then turns and does the same to Elisabeth.

"Do you recognize this woman?"

She is Brandt's mother. She's my mother. Her embrace said it all.

Before I have a moment to process this realization, I am forced into a new scene in Brandt's life, still inside his mind. His head feels groggy, but happy. He sits up to find himself naked in Elisabeth's bed, but she isn't beside him. Panicked, he gets out of bed to search for her, only to find her quietly seated at her wash table staring at her reflection. From the window, I can see the tips of the sun's rays peeking over the hilly terrain in the distance. Brandt walks over to her slowly, kneeling to her level. "What is bothering you, my love?" he says.

The brief happiness that was on her face just hours before had morphed into something darker. "I wanted to enjoy this for longer, this feeling with you. I have wanted this for so long; I just want to live in this place with you, a place where we are not going to battle in a few hours."

Brandt's face struggled to keep a smile as he ran his hands through her hair. "We will live our happily ever after. Today will secure our kingdom's respect and allow us to rule with dignity." She nodded softly toward him, lifting her mouth to his.

Just as our lips touch, the scene changes. Brandt and I are still joined in one body. He is riding a horse alongside Elisabeth. I feel the weight of armor shift on his body with each step of the horse. Elisabeth is almost simple looking. Her hair is pulled into a long blond braid that falls down her back; a fur cape covers extensive armor. Her face is determined and solid; her steely eyes focused on the path ahead. She has the same "zoned" look Liv gets when her mind is sharpened, but this was slightly different. Elisabeth looks vengeful. Her eyes are filled with hatred – hatred for the men who took her father.

Hundreds of their countrymen trail them, riding into battle. The sun is just peeking up above the horizon now. Elisabeth halts her horse and her soldiers follow suit. She turns to face her people. Brandt follows, standing by her side as she addresses her army

"I am not my father. I am not the legendary warrior you are proud to fight alongside in battle. But when my father died, you became my people and I will fight for you until my dying breath, as my father did before me. I am honored to lead you into battle this morning. Today, we will take back our kingdom!" Her voice is strong and clear, echoing through the hillside. The speech is met with a symphony of battle cries. Elisabeth's face softens briefly at the sight of her army, rallied together. As we turn to face forward, we are met with a thousand small black dots in the distance moving in unison. *James. What a dick.*

Elisabeth's steely resistance does not waver. If she was scared, she certainly didn't show it. She raises her sword over her head. The crowd falls silent. She looks to Brandt and nods her head with a half-smile. I feel Brandt's heartbeat quicken. Elisabeth looks straight ahead and points her sword at the enemy releasing a guttural cry, a warrior's scream, a Rebel Yell. The horses begin to gallop beneath us. I hear Brandt meet Elisabeth's scream. Hundreds of men charge in our wake. The enemy army is larger than ours. Brandt looks over to Elisabeth, her eyes locked on the front man leading the charge against them. As our armies collide, I see Elisabeth decapitate the horseman in one swift motion. His body drops from the horse, trampled by his comrades.. I am thrust out of Brandt's mind. I watch on the scene from inside the battle, the warriors moving through my invisible existence.

Seeing war from inside the battle is fascinating. Each soldier dances a different step. Some are outwardly fearful, it shows in their quivered brows and hesitant strikes. Others wear a brave mask that slowly begins to slip away as they deepen into battle. Then there are those who are truly hateful; the ones that start the war. Their eyes look like marbles. Their mouths pressed unto a flat line, until they strike, the corners turning upward at the sight of their handy work.

Elisabeth and Brandt are fascinating to watch, dancing their carefully choreographed duet. Their faces are different from the others. They share a determination, a yearning to protect that the others don't. They fight for their country, but most of all, they fight for each other. Slowly, they begin to separate, always keeping a wary eye on one another. Three enemy men surround Brandt, simultaneously striking at his sword and armor. Out of nowhere, Aleksander comes to Brandt's aid, cutting off the sword arm of one man, using it to stab another. With nothing more than a stern nod, Brandt thanks Aleksander.

One after another, the opposing army falls until the remaining men surrender. They lay their weapons down at Elisabeth's feet and kneel, begging for her mercy. She turns back to meet the eyes of her army and raises her sword. Summoning what little breath she has left, she shouts, "Victory!" Her army roars. Elisabeth turns to meet Brandt's exhausted eyes.

"Happily ever after?" he says, a tired smile on his face.

"Happily ever after," she repeats. Elisabeth turns to see the ruin her army has created and is met with a familiar face. James thrusts a dagger into Elisabeth's side, wiggling between her armor. Instinctively, Brandt plunges his sword into James's unguarded chest. "Long live a King," James said with his dying breath.

Elisabeth stumbles, falling into Brandt. He cradles her body, kneeling to the ground. The crowd falls silent, dumbfounded. I am thrust into Brandt's mind once again, viewing her death through his eyes. I feel Elisabeth laying heavy in Brandt's arms. She looks just like Liv in my nightmares. The warmth of her blood spreads across my hands like oil. Brandt is speechless, his mind empty of anything but pain.

"Ki … You …" Elisabeth tries to speak, but her breath is labored. Elisabeth's fingers move within his hand. "I love you, Bran …"

The light is gone from her eyes. What was once an electric blue is now gray as the sea. Brandt is stiff, Elisabeth lifeless in his arms. I feel the familiar burn of tears escaping their gates as he presses his head to Elisabeth's. The warmth is leaving her body. An open hand silently clasps my shoulder. Without looking, I know it is Aleksander. Brandt picks up Elisabeth's body, overlooking her army. Aleksander kneels to Elisabeth, his head bowed toward the ground in respect. One by one, her army drops to one knee. I feel a wave of emotion wash over Brandt's body. He starts to shake, trying to keep it at bay. As Brandt places Elisabeth's body on his horse, he notices a message written in blood on the hand that held Elisabeth's final moments. "King," she wrote.

"Take a moment to rest. This is a very trying lifetime. When you are ready, go to the next important moment within this life."

I take a moment to feel my breath and the scene around me freezes around me. Everything starts to fade as I close my eyes. There is only me now. I can feel my chest moving up and down; the anxiety I held as Brandt melts into nothing. Like a snake shedding skin, I felt new again.

When I feel ready, I open my eyes and am standing at the foot of a pedestal holding two tall thrones. A disheveled man sits in the smaller of the two thrones with a dark bottle in his hand. The other sits empty except for the crown Elisabeth received on her wedding day. A portrait of her hangs on the wall to his right. His eyes are locked with the painting. Brandt is unrecognizable, his fuller physique and long hair obscuring the man I saw just moments before.

"It was commissioned after my death." Elisabeth stands to my right, so real I could reach out and touch her. "It's not really my favorite, but beautiful all the same. He just sits and stares at it all day, like I am going to walk out of the frame and into his arms; like I have been hiding, waiting for an opportune moment to reveal myself. 'Here I am! I faked my death to make you miserable!' " For such an old broad, she was quite sarcastic.

I stare at her, wondering if she could see me or if I could just see her.

"Yes, I can see you. I am not speaking to myself. I was raised better than to waste my wisdom into the air," she said, turning to me.

I freeze; my mind empty. I don't know if it's because she looked so much like Liv or the fact that she was a real-life Queen, but I am shaking in my metaphorical boots. "I'm sorry; I just wasn't expecting to see you. I was expecting to see him ... me … whatever."

"Well, this time it's a bit different. Watch," she said with a small clap. The scene around us fades away into what looks like a dining hall. Brandt sits alone at the head of a long empty table. There is a place setting at each end. A servant brings wine to the empty place setting across from Brandt, then makes her way to him. As she begins to pour wine into his empty glass, he snatches the pitcher from her hands and begins to drink from it. The servant scurries out of the room, flushed. All at once, 15 servants enter the room, placing various food items on the table. It's enough to feed an army.

"It is enough to feed my people who are going hungry outside these castle walls. The ones he swore to protect," she said, responding to my inner monologue.

After the servants serve the empty place setting and Brandt, they hurry out of the room. . Brandt looks at the food on his plate as he takes another sip from the pitcher. Then he focuses on the empty chair in front of him. His eyes have the glaze of a hazy drunk. He becomes enraged as he ceases to find something he's looking for.

"LEMON CAKES!!!" he shouts furiously. A servant

rushes over to the king. "Where are the damn lemon cakes!" he shouts. "You know they are her favorite! You did this on purpose to mock her. Look at her!" he gestures to the empty chair across from him. "How can we have dinner without her lemon cakes?!"

"Yes, your majesty. I will have those out for you and her majesty in a moment," she says and makes her way back to the kitchen.

"Good," he says, his eyes not leaving the empty chair. "My apologies, Elisabeth. They should know better than this by now." Brandt's eyes roll back as he takes a long pull on his wine.

"They called him the 'Mad King.' After my death, he had no drive to rule our people. I watched him for years destroy everything our family worked so hard to keep stable. He needed to help himself, but he couldn't. So he turned the way of cowardice," Elisabeth explained, her eyes still locked on Brandt.

Brandt removes a long dagger from his robe, rubbing it with his hands, admiring the craftsmanship of the handle and the sharpness of the blade. It's stunning, coated in red stones that shimmer against the candlelight. Seemingly without a thought, he plunges it into his abdomen, ending his own life.

My mind raced to my darkest day, the day I craved sweet relief from this world, the day I wanted an end to it all. The reprieve I felt when I decided that the pain was finally going to end was so freeing; I was seduced by the mere thought of it. It was the day before I left for college. That summer had been unbearable. I watched my friends go out and enjoy their last bit of freedom before going off to school while I wallowed in grief.

On August 22, I planned my execution. To this day I don't know how I didn't succeed. I built a cocktail of antidepressants and sleeping pills and washed it down with nearly a bottle Jack Daniels for good measure. I thought that would have done the trick, easy and painless. I would finally be relieved from the daily pain that dragged me through reliving the death of my father every day. I didn't want to wake up to a world without him in it and finally, I wouldn't have to. Instead, I woke up to a puddle of my own vomit, my pharmaceutical cocktail still intact. I don't remember getting sick or even getting into bed. For some inexplicable reason, I'm still here.

"That is your lesson from this life, Nate. You cannot rely on others to make you whole. You must make yourself whole." Her eyes are electric even in death. The similarity to Liv is uncanny. I can't get past it. But she is right. I depend on Liv for my happiness, on Darrin, my mom, my dad. I'm not whole, not by myself.

My mind starts to wander as I see the servant enter the dining quarters with lemon cakes and slowly approach Brandt. As she draws closer, she screams and drops the cakes on the ground, running back through the door. Brandt is slumped over in his chair, his eyes wide open and bloodshot. I wonder if my eyes would have been open had I succeeded.

"It doesn't matter if your eyes were open or closed. You would be dead and you can't make a difference if you're dead. You aren't done here, Nate. There is so much ahead of you. Learn your lesson from Brandt." We both look back at Brandt. "Some parting knowledge before you leave us," she said. "You should have died. You did die."

"I don't understand. If I died, how ..."

"You were saved. Your soul left your body and then was pushed back in."

"How was my soul pushed back into my body?"

"Someone very powerful is looking over you."

"Who?"

"So many questions, Nathan! Reserve some of the mystery for your dreams. Farewell for now, Nathan," she said touching my shoulder softly, forcing me back into the black.

"Follow your mind. Where does it lead you next?" I hear Dr. Rose prompt.

CHAPTER ELEVEN
Alabama, 1968

I see a dark room in front of me, but I don't feel unsafe. Though I am blind to my surroundings, I know I am viewing the scene through his perspective. I hear little movements from every direction. I feel excitement building inside of him. He is holding someone's hand in the darkness, expertly guiding them.

All at once, the lights spring on and twenty people leap out of hiding and scream "SURPRISE!" I turn to my right and hug the woman whose hand I was holding. She has dark skin and the most radiant smile. Her eyes are shining. It's Liv again.

"Happy birthday, baby," he says and kisses her in front of the crowd. Her eyes well in the excitement as she turns to the crowd and starts to greet her guests. His smile getting wider. He had planned this for a long time.

"What is your name in this life?"

I hear my name – not his name, *my* name. "Nate! Nate!" comes from the far corner of the party. I start to freak out and am immediately forced out of his body and into the party. "Nate!" I hear it again. Slowly, I follow my past self toward the call. He hugs the man calling my name, but I can't get a good look at him. As the man shifts into view, my stomach drops. It's my father, my actual father. He is younger, but it is definitely him. Then Nate hugs the woman standing next to my father. My mother.

"Can you see what you look like?"

I have blond shaggy hair and a small semblance of a beard. I am assuming this is the '60s due to the plethora of bellbottoms at this party.

"Thank you guys so much for coming all the way down here for Belle," Nate said to my parents in a Southern accent so deep, it put Darrin's to shame. "She's had a really tough time lately with all that's goin' on and I knew you all being here on her birthday would cheer her up."

"We wouldn't have missed it!" my mom said.

"Weddings, birthdays. I told you, we don't miss the big ones," my dad said.

Belle spots my parents and rushes over to them with a huge hug. "I can't believe you all are here! How did you get here so quickly?"

"Nate has been planning this for months," my dad said. "We have had this trip booked a while. Plus, we really missed you guys."

Belle was looking into Nate so deeply I thought she could see through him. She was trying to speak, but the words weren't coming out, so he spoke first.

"I love you, Belle," he said, kissing her forehead. "I love you so much that I made someone else host your party so I don't have to clean." Belle erupted into laughter. "Go! Mingle!" Nate said. The scene is changing.

"Can you describe where you are?"

There is a parked car. Belle and Nate are inside of it. Nate kisses her and hops out of the car to open her door. Nate helps Belle out of the car and spins her into a dance in the middle of the gravel driveway. Belle giggles faintly, following Nate's lead. They are silent for a while, just taking in the moment.

The harsh glare of two bright spotlights blind the couple, interrupting their private ball. Something feels wrong. The scene is changing again.

"Tell me what is happening now and describe your surroundings."

Nate and Belle have their hands tied behind their backs and are seated on a white couch that looks out of place in the small home. It might have been a wedding gift from a wealthy relative. Both of them are bleeding, but still conscious. Three men in white hoods surround them, talking to each other, laughing.

"What the hell was this guy thinking takin' up with a nigger like her?" one of the hooded men said.

Nate's mind is cloudy and his eyes are swollen and bruised. He rolls his head to the left see Belle. Her chin is buried in her chest and her breathing is labored, but there.

"Oh, I don't know Mike. She is mighty pretty, for a nigger," the second one said, tracing his fingers up Belle's thigh.

"Stop," Nate said weakly.

"Stop! What are you gonna do about it, nigger lover?" he said, continuing his hand up Belle's thigh.

Summoning every last ounce of life he had left, Nate tackled the man, his hands still tied behind his back, biting as hard as he could into the man's face until his white hood was stained red. A curdling scream leapt from beneath the hood. As Nate backed onto his knees in an attempt to stand, the third man kicked him down, placing his foot on Nate's neck.

"Just for that, you get to watch your little nigger activist housewife get put back in her place." The third man stepped off of Nate's neck, which was quickly replaced by another heavy foot. He picked up a wooden baseball bat, aiming it at Belle's head, mocking the act by imitating Babe Ruth's famous World Series stance.

Nate's neck was pinned to the side, but his eyes are staring into Belle. Belle lifts her head, her eyes small slits amongst a mountain of bruises. She looks at Nate and mouths "I love you." The man with the bat was taking practice swings, stopping just short of Belle's head.

"When's it coming, nigger? Maybe this one?" he would say as he swung. "No, no not that one. We can do better than that!"

"Christ, just do it already! We ain't got all night!" said Mike.

"Alright, alright fine. You got any last words, nigger? Not that anyone will ever hear them, 'cept I guess your nigger-lovin' husband, but he won't be able to pass it on to no one special."

"It was worth it," she said.

"What was worth it? Takin' up with this white boy? Workin' with all them other nigger sympathizers to get King down here to rile up all the rest of you niggers?"

"It was all worth it," she said, staring into Nate's eyes. "Every moment."

"Me too. Me too," Nate could barely get the words out. In one last attempt to free himself, Nate rolls himself out from under the foot of his oppressor and launches himself to his feet, heading straight for the man with the bat.

Before Nate could reach him, the two other men had forced Nate back to knees. The man with bat planted a swing into Nate's stomach, sending him to the floor again, convulsing in pain.

"Well ain't that sweet! Nigger lovers till the end. Well, that's over!" the hooded man with the bat said as he reared it back, smashing it into Belle's head. Again and again he bludgeoned her, pieces of her staining their white outfits. I could barely hear Nate's screaming over the sound of his thoughts. My ears are ringing. I can feel tears running down my face, real tears. After what seemed like hours, the hooded man finally stopped

The killer kneels down beside Nate, Belle's blood dripping from his clothing. "Let's let this one live. I betcha he won't be marchin' in no protests now," he said with a sickening chuckle. Then he brought his face to within inches of Nate's and removed his hood, revealing his hate filled eyes. " 'Bama don't take too kindly to nigger sympathizers. Tell your friends."

"Do you recognize this man?"

He looks familiar, like a nameless face on television, but I don't know him.

"Dammit, Chet!" Mike shouted angrily. "Why the hell did you take your hood off? Now he knows who you are!"

Chet stopped and turned to his hooded accomplice. "Well, then I guess my battin' practice paid off." With that, the hooded man stepped off Nate's neck and Chet brought the bat down on his head. Lights out. It was over quickly for Nate, but Chet kept wailing away, just as he had with Belle.

The scene is changing again, but only to reveal daylight. The hooded men are gone, only Belle and Nate's bodies remain. *Why am I still here? Haven't I seen enough?* There is a knock at the door.

"Nate? Belle?" a man's voice says. "Hey, you guys missed lunch! I am sure you are just canoodling after an amazing birthday party, but damn, call your friends!" he said. "Guys? I know you're in there. Your car is out front. You're not foolin' anyone!" he said, still laughing.

"Come on, let's just go in," a woman's voice whispers.

The door opened with a creak and my parents walked through the door. "Nate! Oh my God, no!" I watched them both run over to Nate and Belle's bodies, their faces unrecognizable from the beatings. My mother is kneeling next to Belle weeping, checking her wrist for a pulse, knowing she wouldn't find one. My father is holding Nate's hand, talking silently to him, almost neurotically.

"Nate, wake up. Please wake up, Nate. Please wake up," he repeated silently.

My mother touched my dad's hair, "They're gone. They're gone, Dennis."

His face turned angry, hateful, like someone flipped a switch inside of him. "We can't let them get away with this. Not this. This isn't a fucking water fountain or a bathroom. These are our friends. We can't let them win." He got up and headed toward the kitchen and picked up the phone on the wall. To the right of him was a photograph of the four of them taped to the refrigerator, arms around each other and smiling. My father took the photo and put it in his pocket as he dialed the police. He turns to my mother who is still seated on the floor, covered in a mixture of their blood.

"You didn't deserve this," she whispers, oblivious to the fact she is covered in blood. "You were good people.

Loving people. Loved people. You didn't deserve this."

I walk over and sit beside my mother. She is crying silently. I reach to comfort her, but just as my hand is about to touch her shoulder, I am forced out, back into the black.

"Follow the path in front of you back into this room. With each breath, you get closer to consciousness. I will count back from five and when I am done you will be here in the present. Five...four...three...two...one."

My face is soaked. My eyes are swollen and raw. I'm still crying. I can't seem to stop. I look over at Dr. Rose. Her eyes are as red and swollen as mine feel. She can't seem to speak yet. Neither of us can. We just sit there in silence for a while, letting our minds catch up with what just happened.

"How were they there, Doc? How were my parents there? Why was his name my name?" I said, finally.

After a moment, when she found the ability to speak, Dr. Rose replied, "I think it would be wise to speak with your mother, Nathan." *Wow, she really must be thrown off. She never calls me by my first name.*

"Are you okay, Dr. Rose?"

"Yes, yes I'm sorry. That time period just hits close to home for me, as it does for many of my generation. I was still living in London during the civil rights movement, but I watched it on television. I remember thinking that it was staged; that there was no way those things could happen in a free country." I could see her mind starting to trail, then refocus. "You should speak with your mother, Mr. James. She may not hold all of your answers, but you might get some clarity about what you saw."

CHAPTER TWELVE

Escape

Walking out of Dr. Rose's office, I started to feel nauseous. The smell of street garbage and hot dogs flooded my nostrils. Passersby run into me, one after another, like I'm not even there. I can't get my mind to focus. I feel my sweat run cold. My chest is tight, struggling for oxygen. The massive hands of this city find a home around my neck, squeezing tighter with each step away from its center. I don't know where I'm going, but it has to be away from here. I feel the fingers tighten around my windpipe at the sheer thought of leaving. I walk into the first car rental place I see.

"Round trip or one way?"

"What?"

"Round trip or one way?"

"Round trip, please."

"ID."

As the clerk processed my information, I fumbled through my phone, but everything just ran together on the screen in a mess of technicolor.

"Economy, compact, intermediate?"

"Whatever is cheapest."

"Economy then."

Within 15 minutes, I was sitting in the driver's seat of a small, red car and staring blankly at 87 Street. I had no idea where I was going. I turned on to Lexington Avenue, and before I could catch my breath, had made my way up the FDR onto the George Washington Bridge. My mind was quiet for the first time in months. I focused on the soft leather of the steering wheel beneath my fingertips and the sound of cars whizzing by me outside the cracked car window. The breeze floated through me, stroking me to ease. I felt a unique sense of control over my life for the first time in years. The scent of freshly cut grass filled my nostrils as I inhaled a long, deep breath. The city's grip around my neck peeled away, finger by finger, as I drove further from the city.

Living in New York is like being in an abusive relationship. It's toxic. You know it's toxic, but for some reason, you love it anyway. You come back, time and time again, no matter how hard it knocks you down. You sit quietly in a pool of your own blood night after night, but still you come back for more. It becomes routine. Rent rising higher and higher, more competition moving into the city every day, ripping away your chances at the dream you came to achieve. There is no ease in living here, so why do we find it so captivating? We live for those unique moments of whimsy, but as the city grows larger and more corporate, that majestic element dwindles. The promise of something more than where we came from keeps us coming back for more punches. But I don't know how many more rounds I have left in me.

I didn't have a plan. I didn't know how long I would drive or where I was going. The sun was going down on my right, lighting a pink and gold fire in the sky. I relaxed into the leather seat. I had escaped.

I heard a buzzing in my pocket. Without looking, I launched the phone out of the window. I felt cleaner, almost primitive, without the burden of the technology. I'm only focused on the road ahead. The sun sank slowly until I saw something I had not seen since I moved to New York: stars.

CHAPTER THIRTEEN

Home

I sat in front of my house staring at the clock on the dashboard. I couldn't say how I got there. My mind was completely free of thought. I had been floating like an unanchored balloon since I left New York. Finally, my feet hit the ground. I knew I was supposed to be there at that moment. I let the positive feeling flood my insides. I'd missed that sense of home.

Fumbling for my house keys, I opened the door slowly, hoping not to wake up my mother. The familiar growl of my stomach disturbed the quiet darkness inside the house. I hadn't eaten since before I went to Dr. Rose's office earlier in the afternoon. Carefully, one light foot at a time, I crept into the kitchen to grab something to eat. Before I could flip on the light, I heard another set of footsteps.

"I hope you're right with God boy, because I'm about to knock your lights out!"

"Mom?"

"Nathan?"

I switched on the light to reveal my mother in her night

clothes holding a crowbar.

"Jesus H. Christ Nathan! I almost beat you to death! What the devil are you doing here at this time of night?"

She was breathing so hard I thought she might be having a panic attack.

"Mom! It's okay, it's okay. Sorry I should have called first."

"Oh, ya think? What's gotten into you?"

"I'm sorry, Mom, really," I apologized opening my arms to give her a hug.

"Well, I can't say I'm unhappy to see you," she said with a light-hearted chuckle. "But, really – What the hell are you doin' here at this time of night?"

I wanted to tell her everything, right then and there, but it was 3 a.m., and my hunger was louder than my eagerness for answers.

"Can we talk about it in the morning? I'm just starving right now and I know you're tired."

"Let me make you somethin', sweetie. What do you want?"

"I will just grab something from the fridge. Do you have any of that chicken salad you make?"

"You know I do! Alright, well, you help yourself and then you will regale me with your story of how you got here. I'm glad you're home, son. I've missed you," she said, giving me a hug and a kiss before heading back to bed.

I devoured a tub of chicken salad and Melba toast and washed it down with a glass of blue Gatorade I'd left during my last visit. After I finished eating, the fatigue hit me. There was something comforting about being back home, sleeping in my bed. Everything was in the same place from my last visit. I grabbed some pajamas from the top drawer. For the first time in months, I slept soundly.

I awoke the next morning to the smell of bacon and black coffee. My mother always spoiled me with home cooking when I was in town. Partly because she missed cooking for someone other than herself, and partly because she wanted to lure me into moving back to Richmond. She routinely made my favorite meals for breakfast, lunch and dinner. This morning, she'd prepared a standard Southern breakfast of bacon, eggs, hash browns, grits, homemade cinnamon buns and black coffee. All better than any restaurant could offer.

"Hey, Sug! How'd you sleep?"

"Like the dead. What time is it?"

"Almost noon, but I figured you would want to get some sleep, considering how late you got in."

We ate in silence for the first few minutes, but I could feel my mother's eyes on me with every bite.

"So are you gonna tell me what's goin' on with you or do we have to play 20 questions?"

"Can we talk about it after breakfast? I'm kind of in the zone here."

"My only child does not just show up out of nowhere at 2:30 in the morning, scarin' the livin' day lights out of me and not provide an explanation. You've gotta give me somethin' here."

My mother has two types of Southern accents: The first, a long, beautiful drawl reminiscent of "Gone with the Wind." She uses it to coerce people into doing just about anything she wants. Fortunately, she only uses this power for good – unlike other Southern women, including my high school girlfriend, who used it to try and buy beer from a local gas station, nearly getting us arrested. The second Southern accent is slightly abrasive and similar to the Beverly Hillbillies. She saves that one for when she runs out of niceties…and patience. Trust me when I say, no one wants to be on the other side of that one. Guess which she was using with me this morning?

"Ma, come on, can't we talk after breakfast? You spent so much time making it. I would hate for it to get cold," I said, making a desperate play at her heartstrings.

"Don't you pull that crap with me, Nathan Alexander James," she said, evading my flattery. "Spill."

She used the middle name. Shit just got real.

"Where did my name come from, Mom?" I said without looking up from my plate.

"Nathan don't try to change the subject. Now tell me …"

"Where did it come from, Mom?" I said, cutting her off.

She shifted uncomfortably. "I don't know, I think your father and I found it in a baby name book or something. Why are you so interested in your name all of a sudden? What is this all …"

"Mom, I know that's not true. I know about Nate and Belle. Now, are you going to give me some answers about this?"

She opened her mouth to speak, but her breath was caught in her throat.

"How … how do you know about them?" she said, dumbfounded by my statement.

"Mom, I didn't mean to upset you. I just need some answers."

"Okay," she said calmly, slowly getting up from the

table. "You finish your breakfast. I need to get a few things together. Is this why you're here, Nathan?"

"Honestly, Mom, I have no idea why I'm here."

She nodded and headed up the stairs.

CHAPTER FOURTEEN

Victoria James

I finished my breakfast and washed the dishes before meeting my mother in the living room. The rule in our house is the cook never cleans. My father found a brilliant way around this rule when he was not in the mood for doing dishes: "We are all going out to dinner tonight! My treat!" It worked every time.

My mom sat on the long couch in the living room, sifting though a box full of papers. I took a seat on the ground, crossed legged, like a child waiting for a story.

"This is your name story, Nathan. Your father and I had plans to tell you this story together before you left for college, but when he got sick – I just couldn't find the strength to tell you myself after he died. I am not ashamed of it, it's just difficult to relive something like this."

"I know what happened to them, Mom. I don't need answers about that. I just want to know where you and Dad fit in to all this. I mean, I saw you guys there that night at the birthday party and then …"

"What do you mean you saw us?" she asked.

"Mom, I have a lot to explain, I know that, but I want to hear what you have to say first."

"Okay, I'll start from the beginning," she said begrudgingly. "You know your father and I met in college, at the University of Alabama, when we were 19. What you probably don't know is that the university had been recently desegregated. That was part of what drew your father and me to the school. Funny enough, we were both at the first protest I ever attended, but we didn't know it at the time. It was very small, barely even made the local paper. We wanted to be a part of integration. We went to protests, volunteered with local civil rights groups, even started an on-campus organization, which didn't make us very popular among certain groups, but we knew what we were getting into.

I met Nate only a few days after I met your father. He was your father's best friend from home, he lived the next farm over from your grandparents. The two of them were the crux of the unbeatable Waverly High School football team. So, naturally when they were both offered football scholarships to the University of Alabama, they decided they couldn't break up such an unstoppable duo. They were inseparable. They roomed together, studied together, goofed off together. You remember how funny your father was? Imagine him having an equally as funny, blonde brother – that was Nate. So as you can imagine, Nate's approval was vital to our relationship.

I met Belle even before I met your father. We were roommates our freshman year. I will never forget the day we met for the first time. I had gotten to our room first and set up my things on one side of the room. I knew the name of my roommate, but no other information was given to me. I waited for hours to meet her. Finally, I decided to leave the room, only to see this woman standing at the end of the hall. She was slender, but very tall, at least four inches taller than me, but from the way she stood cowered at the end of the hall, you would think we were the same height. She looked lost, so I offered to help her find her room."

"Oh, thanks, I know where it is," Belle said, without looking me in the eye.

"Well, can I help you with your stuff? I'm Victoria! I'm in room 214."

"I'm in room 214 …" she said with her eyes downcast.

"Oh! Belle! It is so nice to meet you! I have some ideas for the room, if you're into decor. I brought a ton of prints, but I wanted to get your opinion before I put them up. Oh! Also, I brought a record player with tons of records. What kind of …"

"I asked for a black roommate. I'm so sorry. I can go get reassigned," she said, still not looking at me.

"Why would you get reassigned? Is it the prints? We don't have to put them up! I just brought them in case …"

"Because I'm black and you are white. I think they made a mistake. I don't want to cause any trouble."

"Honestly, Nate I felt like the biggest idiot on the planet. Here I am motor-mouthing about the damn walls, and all she is worried about is being able to stay in school."

"Well, I don't think they made a mistake. The school is desegregated, so that means you and me are roomies and you have to help me figure out how to decorate our humble abode," I said, but she didn't look convinced. "Look, Belle, I don't care about what color you are, but I will care if you snore. What do you say we get to know each other over a bottle of wine I stole from my parents?"

"I don't snore, and I prefer bourbon. I took some from home, too," she said, loosening up slightly.

"I think this is going to be the start of a beautiful friendship," I said laughing.

"Belle and I became very fast friends and she snored like a freight train every night. It became our longest running inside joke. She loved the prints I brought and even brought some of her own. She was brilliant. Belle was the whole reason I passed my science requirement in college. She was my best friend.

After I met your father, we devised a plan to get Nate and Belle together. The four of us decided to meet in the campus café for dinner after our last class on Friday. Your father and I quickly swore off ever playing matchmaker again after that night. Belle and Nate spent the entire evening arguing. They butted heads on everything from new scientific discoveries to art theory. But I think that was the spark that ignited the fire. Neither of them had ever met someone that could keep up with them. They fell head over heels for each other, during an argument as a matter of fact, and that was it. They got married when they were 20 years old, still in college, and your father and I got married shortly after that. Belle and Nate stayed very involved in the civil rights movement, as did we, but it meant something much bigger to them. It meant they could hold hands in public without being ridiculed or have dinner at a restaurant together without being turned away.

On March 7, 1965, before we were married, your father, Nate, Belle and I were ready to march from Selma to Montgomery for voting rights. That day was later dubbed 'Bloody Sunday.' The march was blocked by the police before we could even get out of Selma. Nate and Belle worked very closely with Dr. King's group to arrange the march, they even got to meet him before the protest. We were only sophomores in college at that point – we were babies.

When things started to turn bad, we were right in the middle of it. It was such a blur. I can remember the burn of the tear gas in my throat, choking me. I couldn't breathe, I couldn't see. I could hear screaming from every direction. All at once, I felt your father, throwing me over his shoulder and running me out of the line of fire. I saw the blurred figures of Nate and Belle trailing in our wake. I watched a blurry uniformed man smack Belle across the cheek with a billy club. A second later, I hear a crack. Nate had broken the man's nose and pulled Belle on to his back, running behind us. When we were finally out of the crowd, we could barely breathe. The four of us sat curled in an alley nearby to escape the chaos, listening to the screams of our fellow protesters, helpless to do anything.

When we finally got our senses back, we took Belle to the nearest hospital, which turned us away. We went to a clinic, and they turned us away. We tried everywhere we could think of, but we were turned away. I had made friends with a pre-med student on campus earlier that year, and luckily he helped us out when we arrived back to campus. Belle was fine physically, but we were all pretty shaken from the experience.

The march finally happened after several attempts on March 21, 1965, but we did not attend. Belle wanted to go, but in the end, Nate convinced her not to:"

"Belle, this is worth fighting for, but it's not worth your

life, and I refuse to lose you to this. If you decide to go, I will walk beside you until my legs fall off, but I'm scared. I can't lose you, Belle. I won't be able to survive it."

"I know that makes us sound like cowards. I thought we were cowards. It is still one of my biggest regrets. Things settled down after that. We still worked with various civil rights groups and attended protests, but we were never in that position again."

She paused for the first time since her story began. Her eyes are starting to well up.

"I just need a minute," she said, staring into the box of papers. I nodded, silently giving her the space she needed.

"I never wanted to have to tell you this story, you know. I don't think I have ever told this story out loud before. In a way, I'm kind of glad you already know the outcome. The birthday party that Nate threw for Belle came a year or two we graduated. Your father and I had moved to New York right after college for internships. Nate and Belle had put roots down in Alabama when they bought a home just outside of Montgomery. Belle was from Alabama and her mother was ill, so she wanted to be close to home.

When Nate called us about the birthday party, we thought it was a little odd. It wasn't a big birthday and it cost an arm and a leg for us to get down there, especially on our meager salaries. Nate said that things were getting worse for them down there. They couldn't leave the house together without being threatened. Nate even bought their house posing as an unmarried man just so they would get approved for a loan. The desperation in his voice was heartbreaking. I believe you know the rest and I would prefer not to relive that part unless you have any specific questions about it."

I had never seen my mother this defeated. She looked like she did at my father's funeral, hardened, trying not to cry. I climbed on the couch and wrapped my arms around her. As if tapping cracked glass, she broke. I just sat there, holding her for the longest time, not saying a word.

"You would have loved them, Nathan. They were wonderful people. Your father and I discussed having children right after we got married and wanted them to be the Godparents. After they were killed, we couldn't imagine being parents − We didn't want to bring a child into a world where something so awful could happen to people as wonderful as they were. Don't take this the wrong way, because we were over the moon when we got pregnant, but you were a little bit of a surprise to us." She smiled for the first time since we started our conversation.

"Mom, did they ever find out what happened? Like who did it?"

Her face went cold again.

"After we called the police, we stayed until they arrived. They asked us a million questions, even accused us of committing the murder, but we were out with a group of friends the night before, after Nate and Belle left the party, so we were cleared. Your father and I stayed in Alabama for two weeks after, keeping up with the investigation and helping Nate and Belle's parents with the service arrangements.

The Birmingham police department investigated for a total of 48 hours, then brushed it off as a robbery gone wrong. Nate's death made the front page of the papers, Belle barely had a footnote. They referred to her in the paper as, 'the victim's negra friend.' When it came to arranging the service, Belle's mother suggested they have separate services so they wouldn't draw too much attention. Nate's mother, who was never fully on board with her son's interracial marriage, disagreed, shocking us all.

"Our kids died because they loved each other, we both know that in our heart of hearts," Nate's mother said to Belle's Mother. "Black or white, that's somethin' that deserves rememberin'."

"I never liked that woman, but in that moment, I loved her.

The service was beautiful. Mrs. Haze, Nate's mom, decked the place out with the most beautiful flowers. She even sat next to Mrs. Beauford, Belle's mother, at the service. Your father and I gave the eulogy, I think they would have liked that. They were laid to rest, side by side, in Belle's hometown. Mrs. Haze put up a fight at first to have Nate laid to rest in Virginia, but she came around eventually. They deserved to be buried together. The geography of it was such a small detail in the end."

Mom paused and took in a deep breath, exhaling the weight of her history from her lungs. "Well, that's the story, Nathan. So are you going to let me in on how the hell you know about all this?"

I sighed, mentally preparing myself to relay a story that I didn't even know if I believed. "Okay, but it is going to sound crazy. Just keep an open mind, okay?" Over the next hour, I told mom everything. I told her about Jackson and Brandt, I told her about losing my job, I told her about how I saw Nate and Belle, about how I feel like I have lost my lust for art. I confessed everything. It felt good to tell someone else about what I had experienced.

It's been festering inside since my first regression.

"So you're telling me," she spoke finally, trying to talk through her thoughts, "that you're Nathan Haze?"

"Mom, I know it sounds weird …" Before I could finish my thought I was wrapped in a hug. I could feel the warmth of her tears through my T-shirt. When she pulled away, she was smiling.

"I know I shouldn't feel this way, but I almost feel comforted. Like their lives weren't for nothing."

"So, wait, you actually believe in all this, Mom?"

"Of course I do!"

"But you and Dad were never religious. I thought you didn't believe in anything that had to do with the afterlife or God?"

She took a long pause, like she was finding the best way to string her thoughts together. "After Belle and Nate were killed, your father and I searched for answers everywhere, something to justify what had happened to our friends. We read the Bible, but all we found were holes in the Christian fabric. Ultimately, we were mad at God, mad that all the Sundays we spent listening to a man preach His word could never offer an explanation as to why good people are taken from this world before their time.

"That is when your father and I decided to look outside the religion we were both raised on, and we started exploring alternative beliefs. We studied Islam, Buddhism, Hinduism, Judaism, all of which have similar themes and stories. Your father and I decided that instead of forcing one belief on you, we would allow you to make your own decision, just as we did."

"So, what do you believe in, Mom?"

"I believe that something as large as creation and re-creation can't be captured in a simple text written by flawed men. There will always be something we can't explain, something that we blindly believe in simply because we have faith. I believe that if you live your life well on this Earth – with kindness, love, happiness and charity – you spread goodness that stays long after you're gone. I don't know what an afterlife entails or what will happen there, but I do believe there is something larger at play. Something that watches over us and aids in our destinies, pushing us toward the right answer, but it's up to us to take the hint. What you told me about reincarnation fits right into that belief. I have always thought that I would see your father again, in one way or another. Hearing your experience confirms that for me, it comforts me. Death is just a pit stop."

"How does Liv feel about all this? She seems to be a large part of these lives. I'm sure she is intrigued by what all this means," Mom said, slyly switching the subject back to me.

Liv. I hadn't even stopped long enough to call her after my disappearance.

"I haven't talked to her since I left."

"Did you two have a fight?"

"No, nothing like that. I just … I just left."

"Nathan Alexander. You left that girl without even a wave in the rear-view mirror? I know I did not raise you to be that disrespectful."

"Mom, it wasn't like that. When I left, I wasn't even thinking about Liv, I was only thinking about myself and what I'd seen. I felt trapped. I just had to get out of New York. I needed to find clarity. There was nothing and no one else on my mind. I didn't even plan to end up here, it just kind of happened. I was really shaken up, ya know?"

"Has she tried to call you since you've been gone?"

"Well, probably. I don't really know."

"How do you not know?" she asked.

"Well, I kind of threw my phone out the window on my drive here," I responded shamefully.

"Nathan, you are in a mess of trouble with that girl. I cannot believe you would do that to someone, let alone the girl you claim to love!"

"I know, Mom, I know. I messed up. I will fix it."

"Well, from everything you have told me about those past people you were, it seems you all have the same problem: You keep messin' it up with your girl. The other times, it couldn't be helped, but this time, it's just you being an idiot. You need to sit down and have a good think about yourself because this is not the Nathan that I raised."

"Yes ma'am," I said reflexively, and left to go to my room.

"Nathan," mom called after me. "Call that girl. I can't imagine what she is feeling right now."

"Yes, ma'am." I picked up the landline, but before I could dial the numbers, the phone started to ring.

"Hello?"

"Nate?"

"Liv!"

"Nate, what happened! What are you doing at home? I was just going to call your mom to see if she had heard from you! When you didn't show up to the exhibit last night, I tried to call you, but your phone was dead. What the hell, Nate?" she said. I could hear the anger increasing in her voice.

"Liv, I'm fine. I just … I just had to get out."

"Out of where? Out of the house? Out of this relationship? What did you need to get out of?"

"No, no! I just needed to get out of New York for a while. Just to clear my head."

"What happened, Nate?"

"I went back to see Dr. Rose again." She was silent. "Some things came up and they really scared me. I felt this overwhelming urge to leave."

"And you couldn't give me a courtesy call?"

"Honestly, I didn't even think about it. I was so overwhelmed, all I could think was that I needed to leave."

"What did you see?" she asked softly, like she was talking to a child.

"I don't really want to talk about it, Liv. It's still a lot to process. Can I …"

"Nate," she said sighing, exhausted from answer, "You never want to talk about what's bothering you. You let it build and build inside until it consumes you and you do something like leave your girlfriend and your best friend in the world worried that you're dead in a ditch somewhere. You can't do this to people. Take responsibility for your actions and stop blaming the world for your problems."

"Liv …"

"I have to call Darrin and let him know your okay. He has been running around to every corner of the city looking for you."

"Liv, please wait …"

"Bye, Nate." Liv had never been mad at me before. Maybe a few times for not picking up my clothes off the floor or leaving dirty dishes in the sink, but never like this.

I knew I needed to go back to New York and fix this.

"Mom, I'm going to head back if that's okay."

"Was that Liv?"

"Yeah …"

"You better fix this, kiddo. You have never been better than when you were with that girl and you know it." Her logic was irrefutable.

"I will, mom. I love you," I said giving her a hug and a kiss goodbye.

"Nate," she said as I turned to walk away. "There is one more thing I want to ask you, which you might not be able to answer. When you saw this happen to Nate and Belle, did you see what their attackers looked like?"

I gave it a moment, retracing that memory in my mind. "Chet. One of the guys, he took off his hood and his name was Chet. He had shaggy dark hair, kind of a big guy. Does that mean anything to you?"

She thought a moment, then shook her head. "Not that comes to mind. Maybe if I look through some of this stuff I can figure it out." She looked pensively at the stack of memories.

"Oh! I forgot. Before you go, I wanted to give you something," she said rummaging through the box. She handed me a folded piece of paper. "This was taken right after Belle and Nate got married. Your father …"

"Dad took this off the refrigerator the day you found Nate and Belle."

"Yes," she said, still a bit in shock. "Well, get home safe, son. Love you."

"Love you, Mom," I said, putting the picture in my pocket.

CHAPTER FIFTEEN

Detour

About an hour into my trip, the exit for Petersburg, Virginia pulled me to the off ramp. I hadn't been to my grandparent's farm since I was a kid, but that day I was aching to return. I wanted to sit in my tree, the tree I used as my happy place for the regressions. Since my grandparents passed away, the farm has been vacant. It's in the middle of nowhere, so there wasn't a real threat of vandals or thieves, not that there is much to steal anyway.

When I arrived, the property looked just the same as it always had from a distance, minus the flourishing crops in the front fields, but when I drew closer, I noticed it's weakened condition. The barns had been ravaged by years of storms and the house was overgrown with neglect. I walked to my favorite barn, the one that held the antique tractor. I opened the door and was met with an army of dust mites and flies. When the air cleared, I surveyed the the contents of the garage. Precious knick knacks and old tools still littered the walls, unloved for decades. I traced the letters of an old license plate with my fingers, remembering a time when it was tacked safety to the front of my grandfathers tractor.

I walked over to the main house which looked as it had forever, pecans still scattered on the ground waiting to be picked and shucked, the apple trees still growing the sporadic fruit, and my tree still stood in all her glory at the rear of the house. I used to have so much fun watching my family look for me frantically, when all they had to do was look up. They would get so mad when they heard me snickering from above. "Nathan Alexander James! Do you find our worrying amusing? Get your butt down outta that tree right this instant before I whoop it with the nearest switch I can find!" Mom would say, my dad trying to withhold his laughter behind her.

The tree is just as huge as I remembered, her branches still green and weepy. I climb up to the top, just as I had so many times before. There is a piece in the middle where two huge arms of the tree connect, creating the most wonderful seat for daydreaming. The spot holds the most perfect view of the sky, her branches framing the clouds as they float by in a picture show of shapes. Everything is so quiet. No sirens, no people yelling in the street, not even the blare of a car radio can find me here. I start to do the breathing exercises Dr. Rose taught me. I close my eyes and take in the moment. The stress melts away. Before I know which way is up, I feel myself slipping into the black without the safety net of Dr. Rose's guidance. I'm on my own. To my surprise, I didn't land in another life. I'm still lying peacefully in my tree.

The world looked just as it did before I fell into the black. A light breeze still brushing the branches of my tree, the sun on my face. The foliage looked more brilliant than it did when I was awake. The trees were greener, apples more red. I looked below and saw a man staring up at me, eating an apple. His face was shielded by a large straw hat. As he lifted his eyes to mine, I knew immediately that he was my father. He turned to walk away into the crop field, now alive with rows upon rows of corn, just as I remembered it growing up. Without thinking, I launched myself from the tall tree, but I hit the ground lightly, like I was attached to bungee cord. I start running toward him, but the faster I ran, the more distance grew between us.

Defeated, I stopped and sat down in the field, exhausted. Just like the dreams, I lost him again. My head fell heavy into my hands. I felt a tap on my shoulder and looked up. There was a large staircase in the middle of the field, surrounded by light. I ran toward it. When I got to the base, I immediately recognized it as the staircase from my childhood home. I lifted one foot to climb the stairs, but something weighed me down, keeping me from taking a step.

"Take that off, Son," I heard a voice say from the top of the stairs.

"Take what off?"

"That backpack, it's holding you back."

I felt the familiar pull of two straps on my shoulders and was suddenly aware of its weight. I could barely stand. Carefully, I removed the backpack and instantly felt relieved. In the distance, I noticed someone peeking around the corner upstairs, waiting for me.

"Well, come on now!" I heard him say.

I climbed the stairs slowly, one foot at a time. As I approached the top, the figure came into view. It was my dad, looking just as I remembered him. His glasses, his kind smile, his beard, all the same as in my favorite memories with him.

"Hey, kiddo. I've been waiting for you," he said, holding his arms out toward me. I ran right into them without hesitation, like I did as a child when he would come home from work. I felt like I was six years old again. I could actually feel his arms wrapped around me, he even smelled the same. It was overwhelming.

"Dad? Is this really you? Is this really happening?" I could feel my voice quivering.

"Yeah, buddy. It's really me, I'm here," he said hugging me tighter. "I missed you, Nathan." Words eluded me. All I could feel was happiness. I didn't want to let go of him. "Sorry to ambush you like this, but my other messages were getting through to you."

"What messages?" I said sitting on the floor in front of him. We were now surrounded by my childhood home. We were seated on the balcony overlooking the living room, my room just ahead at the end of the hall, just the same as it was when I was young.

"You didn't think you were just seeing that stuff for fun did you? I was hoping that would knock you into shape, but I guess you needed a little more of a push."

"What, do you mean the past lives? Yeah, I think I have had enough of that after the last one, thanks."

"Well, get ready, because you're not done yet," he said eerily.

My mind was going in a million different directions. I had so many questions, but none of them came to mind. "Dad, how am I seeing you?"

"The same way you saw all of your lives. You allowed

your mind to go to the place in between this world and the next. Here, your mind shows you what you need to see to benefit you in your current path."

"So, is this real? Am I really seeing you or are you just something my mind made up?"

"I'm very real, just as everything you saw with Dr. Rose was real."

"How did you know about …"

"You didn't think Liv just stumbled upon the good doctor, did you?" he said with a knowing smile. "I had been trying to get you two there for quite some time, more you than she."

"But why? Couldn't you just magically make that happen? Don't you have any perks up here?"

"It doesn't really work like that," he said laughing. "You have to be open to the experience, something you definitely were not. I probably pushed harder than I was supposed to, but I knew it would be worth it."

"Why did you show me that stuff? I can't fix it, so what's the point? I mean, it's cool seeing everything from the past, but what am I supposed to do with all that now? I feel more confused now than I did before knowing about all this."

"You needed to see your mistakes in other lives so you wouldn't repeat them in this one. You stormin' off on Liv and Darrin isn't exactly helping your case. You three have been traveling together for over 60 lifetimes and you still can't seem to get it right."

"What do you mean? Darrin and I are fine and Liv will get over it when I explain everything."

"That's just it, Nathan. You depend on them to just forgive you, feeding them excuses as to why you do the things you do. Eventually, the excuses will run out and you will find yourself without the most important people in your life. Your actions affect other people. Darrin needed you when I died, but you secluded yourself away until you ran off to college,, and even tried to kill yourself. How do you think Darrin's life would have been had you succeeded? Not to mention your mother's? And don't even get me started on Liv! She has done everything possible to motivate you, to keep you from falling down, and you still can't give her the partner she needs. Both of them need you just as much as you need them.

I died. I left you and your mother too soon, but that was the life I chose before I was even born into the world. I chose to be with your mother, I chose to have you as my child and I chose Darrin to be your brother from another mother. All of this was predetermined. Our existence is made up of checks and balances. I sacrificed my life in this lifetime to pay a debt for you."

"What debt are you talking about? Why did you have to pay it! I could have done that myself and then you would still be here!" I said angrily.

"Every lifetime that we come back to the physical form is a chance to learn and make amends for another lifetime. The mistakes of other lifetimes are debts that we owe. We can pay the debt for someone else or choose to pay them ourselves. I chose to pay your debt in this life as you have paid mine in numerous lives before. But I'm not here to talk to you about debts; you will understand that in time, that information is unimportant to you now. I'm here to help you with this life, to learn from your past mistakes. You are particularly lost in this lifetime for a variety of reasons. You live behind your excuses, justifying to yourself the reasons why you can't move forward. It has caused you to be selfish in your relationships with the people closest to you, taking advantage of their love. You use my death as an excuse and people continue to accept that because they have never felt the kind of loss you feel. Death is not an excuse for messing up in life. You have an opportunity to use your experience with loss for the betterment of yourself and of others, but you choose to use it as a bartering chip. Focus on all that you have, not the one that you lost. If you only focus on the negative, that is all you will receive in return. You being lost is a result of your refusal to be found. You don't take the chances you should. Instead, you wait for them to fall into your lap, like most things in your life. Not everything comes that easily.

Throughout your lives, you have failed to save Liv because it was out of your control. Now the universe is giving you the chance to make things right, to do what you couldn't in the past, and you push her away, setting yourself up to lose her all over again. Darrin has protected you lifetime after lifetime, but when he needs someone, you fall away."

I imagined my first meeting with my father after his death being a little more rainbows and sunshine and a lot less scolding. But my dad was right, I was being selfish. I nodded my head, agreeing with everything he was saying. I took a moment, reflecting on his word. "What do I do, dad? How do I fix this?"

"If only it were that easy," he said, laughing. "Just trust yourself. Listen to your gut. You will know what to do. Trust yourself to make the right decisions."

"But how do I know …"

"Trust yourself, Nathan. You know exactly what to do."

We sat in a comforting silence for a while. I got the feeling it was time for me to leave, but I wasn't ready. I don't think I could ever be ready to leave him again.

"You can always come back, you know," he said, as if he was reading my thoughts.

"How?"

"Just like you did today. Find the staircase and I will be at the top. This is where I live. When you die, you choose in which part of your life to live, and I chose this time. You were young, around six or seven years old, in this house, just the three of us and Darrin, of course. That was my favorite time. You can find me here whenever you need me."

Suddenly it felt okay, even right to leave. "How do I get back?"

"Just follow the staircase down and walk back to your tree. Easy enough, right?"

I started to feel hesitant, like I was leaving him behind.

"You're not, kiddo. This is where I choose to be. You need to live your life, better the lives of the people around you. I am always with you, Nathan. When you paint, I stand behind you, watching each brushstroke. It makes me so proud to watch your talent come alive. I am always listening if you want to talk. You will know what I'm saying back if you listen hard enough."

As I got up to leave, I gave my father one more hug. "Mom is never going to believe me when I tell her about this," I said, giving dad a sly look.

"Just tell her I did fix the rear tire that time in Philly. She will believe you then."

"What does that even mean?" I asked..

"Just tell her. And tell her I love her with all my heart, even in death. Tell her I like that she still asks me for advice about big decisions. Tell her if she listens closely, she will always hear my answer."

I nodded. "I love you, dad. Thanks for this. It took you long enough!" I said, teasingly.

"Everything comes to you at the right time; you just have to be patient. Nothing is by chance. I love you too, buddy. Remember, if you need me, I'm here," he said with a final hug.

As I got to the bottom of the staircase, I remembered the backpack. "Do I take this with me?" I asked, looking back up at him.

"No, Son. Leave that with me. You won't need it anymore."

"What's in it? It's so heavy, it feels important."

"Those are all your worries and regrets, everything that's been holding you back. You were so attached to them that you never realized their weight. You're not going to need those now. I'll take care of them for you," he said with a nonchalant wave, like he was taking out the trash.

To tell you the truth, part of me wanted to take them with me. It was all I ever knew – the worry, the regrets, the bad feelings. I hid behind those for so long, I felt naked without them. But I trusted Dad.

"Thanks, Dad. See ya later, alligator!"

"After a while, crocodile!"

With a wave and a smile, I walked the path through the crop field back into my tree. When I settled back into my spot, I fell into the black and woke up into a new reality.

CHAPTER SIXTEEN

Facing the Music

When I first crawled into my tree, the sun was shining bright on my face. Now, the sky was turning to twilight. Quickly, I climbed down from my tree and headed toward my car. My head was spinning, like when you stand up too fast. I couldn't get a grip on reality, but I had this unrelenting feeling I needed to get back to Liv. I started the car and watched the farm disappear in my rearview mirror. A feeling of lightness ran through me. I had no fear, no worry for the first time in years. I was free. Five hours later, I returned the rental car and sprinted home. The only thought in my mind was Liv.

I bolted through the door to find Liv curled in her chair, her face toward the living room window. Two small suitcases sat beside her. When her face turned to mine, it was blank. The radiance she carried was gone. The smile she always had for me had faded. I waited for her to say something, but she was quiet. I wished she would scream at me, tell me I'm awful for leaving. At least then I could tell what emotion she was feeling. But she said nothing.

Her eyes looked tired and spoke louder than anything she could say.

After a moment, she stood and walked toward me, leaving a foot of distance between us. "I'm not going to drown with you, Nate," she said finally. "I can't hold back my happiness because you can't find yours. I'm just … I'm just so tired. I'm so, so tired. I can't keep living for both of us."

My throat catches. A familiar burning invades my eyes and cheeks, spreading into my chest. I know what's coming next.

"I can't do this anymore, Nate. I'm sorry, I just can't."

My stomach dropped like a ball of lead.

"I already called Delia and she said I can stay with her for a few days until I find a new place. I will come by to pick up my things later this week," she said.

I can't believe this is happening. She wasn't crying. She wasn't screaming. She wasn't cold. She was broken. I broke her. I could see the pain of exhaustion when she looked at me. That glow I survived on had faded. I had eaten it up. My mind was panicked. I didn't know how to string together the words I needed. My mouth kept opening trying to find something, but there was nothing. The burning in my eyes was too hard to push away now, they were on fire.

As she turned to collect her bags, all I could get out was, "Please, no. Please, no."

She turned and wrapped her arms around me softly, like I might break if she squeezed too hard. My head rested on her shoulder, breathing in her scent. She lifted her mouth to my ear.

"Nate, I love you. I love you so much that I have to let

you find yourself. Until then, we can't be together. Find yourself and then come find me." With that, she peeled me from her shoulder, holding my face in her hands. She looked into my eyes like she could see through them, right down into everything I let build inside of me, everything I wouldn't let her see. She turned my head toward her and kissed my cheek. The door closed.

I collapsed onto the floor, knees tucked to my chest. After all the dreams, all the lives, all the pain I felt when I lost her time and time again, that paled in comparison to this.

I calmed down and pulled myself into Liv's chair. It was still warm from where she had been sitting. I allowed myself to be wrapped in it, wrapped in her. This can't be happening, not after everything we have been through. Not after the thousands of years we have spent together. Maybe that's what the dreams meant. Each one had a definite end for Liv and me, no chance of redemption, no chance of finding her. This was my last chance to find her.

Remembering I have no phone, I ran to the deli across the street and asked to use theirs. The clerk, Joe, and I were on a first name basis due to my infamous caffeine addiction.

"Why do you my phone? Where's your cell?" asked Joe.

"Long story short, at the bottom of the Hudson."

"Okay," John said, handing me the phone. "But don't call overseas or my ass is grass."

"Don't worry, it's domestic," I responded, dialing the phone. Someone picked up almost immediately.

"Office of Dr. Cecilia Rose. How can I help you?"

"I need to speak with Dr. Rose, it's urgent."

"I'm sorry, Dr. Rose is out today, but I would be happy to set you up an appointment for tomorrow?"

"No, I need to speak with her now, this is an emergency."

"Okay, let me see if I can get her on the line. Who is experiencing this emergency?"

"Nathan James."

"Oh. She said to be expecting your call. I will patch you right through. Please hold."

How did she know I was going to call? Did Liv go back and talk to her without telling me?

"Mr. James, I've been expecting your call."

"HOW?!" I said a little too aggressively. "How have you 'been expecting' my call?" I am beating with rage for this woman without reason. Maybe it's Dr. Rose's constant assumptions about the future or the arrogant way she assumes I'm an idiot. My heart is thumping wildly. If I were any madder, my eyeballs would pop out of their sockets.

"They told me you would be calling. Would you like to meet to speak about the events of today?"

"How the hell do 'they' know what happened today? I can't even comprehend what happened today!"

"Mr. James, I've said it once, I've said it a thousand times, there are things in this world that you will just have to accept that you don't or you refuse to understand. Now, would you like to meet or not."

My rage slowly subsides. "Yes. I need to meet with you now."

"I agree, Mr. James. Shall I meet you at your residence? It would be better if we were someplace you feel comfortable and connected."

"Yes. When should I expect you?"

"I was already in route. I will be there in 5 minutes."

Five minutes later to the second, I watched a black SUV pull up outside our apartment building. The buzzer rang followed by a polite knock. I knew it was Dr. Rose. I watched her get out of her car and enter the building, but for some reason I held on to the lingering hope that it was Liv behind that door. Impossible hope, but hope nonetheless. I opened the door to reveal Dr. Rose standing in a flowy dress, straw hat in hand.

"Come on in, Doc." She entered without a word. She observed my apartment, more with curiosity than judgment. "Did you just come from the beach or something?" She wasn't clad in her usual city garb.

"Yes, I was just in the Hamptons."

"The Hamptons are 3 hours from the city, at least. How did you get here so quick?"

"As I said before, Mr. James, I had been expecting your call. Now, shall we get started?" She headed toward Liv's chair to take a seat.

"Not there," I responded almost automatically.

"Yes, I see. Perhaps you should sit in her chair." Dr. Rose sank into our small couch while I took Liv's seat. It feels weird to be here with another woman that isn't Liv, even if it is just Dr. Rose.

She reached inside her straw bag and pulled out a green bundle and lit it on fire. It smelled like her office. "Apologies for the fire Mr. James, but I need to cleanse the area prior to our beginning." I nodded. "You have a very lovely home, you know, very representative of both of you. Typically you see a couple's apartment fall strongly to the masculine or feminine. Your home is quite comforting. I can see why it was so hard for her to leave." I felt my neck ablaze and my heart begin to pound as I watched Dr. Rose walk around the room. "No need to be upset, Mr. James. She left, but she isn't gone."

"How do you know?"

"What did she say to you when she left?" I couldn't remember. It was like those few minutes were a blur, like a dream, or rather a nightmare. "Did she say 'I never want to see your face again as long as I live,' scream and stomp out the door?"

I felt myself smirk. The thought of Liv making a production like that was comical. "No, no she didn't. She did say she loves me. She wants me to find me and then find her."

"Are *those* the words she used now?" Dr. Rose asked with a knowingly look. "How interesting."

I knew the parallel she was drawing; she had been drawing it all along. I just rolled my eyes. "Okay, so what are we doin' here? Same deal? I go back, see Liv die again and hopefully extract some sort of lesson that will save my relationship?"

"Not quite as bluntly as you put it, but yes, something like that. I thought we would start with a regression and see where that leads. They are telling me that this life will be more revealing, I assume because we are in the space you share with Ms. Hammond. Are you ready?"

I nodded and closed my eyes as Dr. Rose took me through the relaxation exercise. Quicker than before, I fell into the black. Usually something appears almost instantly, but this time I was floating for what seemed like forever. I could see scenes of my former lives passing by me, some I had seen before, some I hadn't. I tried to enter one of the scenes that looked to be in the 1920s, but I was pulled back from it, like a mother pulling back a child from traffic. Finally, I am launched into one of the scenes.

CHAPTER SEVENTEEN
Pompeii, 79 A.D.

"Can you tell me where you are, Nathan?"

I could hear Dr. Rose's voice clearly. It is soft and comforting, guiding me through this maze. My soul settles into another vehicle. As my vision sharpens, I run my hands over the thin material covering my body. It is sweltering hot, but I can feel a strong breeze combing through my hair. The air tastes salty. I can hear waves crashing in the distance.

My vision is in full focus now. I've been here before, but only for a moment. This is the incomplete life from my first regression, the one I saw right before Dr. Rose woke me up.

There is a large black cloud in the distance. It looks like it's coming toward me, but no one is paying any attention to it. I see men, women, even children draped in extravagant jewelry, laughing and drinking wine from gilded cups. Servants trail them carrying what look to be large boxes filled with personal items. The sea sits to my right. I have never seen a place so beautiful and alive.

Everyone seems to be a part of one big party. It looks like an ancient version of a Sandals Resort.

"What is your name?"

It starts with a T. Titan or Titus? Titus is my name. My hair is curly and very dark and my skin is a dark bronze.

"Look at your shoes. What do they look like?"

The less fortunate wear nothing more than a burlap sack, their feet dirty from walking barefoot. I am wearing worn leather sandals that tie at the ankle and my clothing is made up of a plain white linen fabric, almost like a dress, cinched at the waist with a belt that looks like a piece of gold rope. I am not adorned with various jewels, nor am I dirty from a hard day's labor. I only wear one dark metal ring on my left hand. Nothing of value, but it is very sentimental. It is my wedding ring, which was given to me by my wife's father. Hers looks the same … identical, actually. It was made from a family heirloom, a sword of some kind with an intricate engraving in the blade.

"What can you tell me about your life here?"

I'm happy. I am not rich, but I am not a slave anymore. I was freed and am beginning to climb the ranks as a merchant. My mentor is to my left. He is very old with white hair and a beard and he walks with a cane. We are standing in front of a small storefront that is crowded with people. Tapestries of all colors hang from the ceiling. They are intricately woven and attract the wealthier people on the island. I can feel Titus's eagerness to count the profit, already thinking of all the ways to spend his share.

"Do you recognize this man from your present life?"

I look closer into the old man's eyes. They are brown

144

with just a touch of gold, making them warm and welcoming. They're my father's. His demeanor is familiar and comforting throughout each lifetime. I have come to count on it.

"Someday, someday soon, this will be yours," the old man says. I can feel Titus becoming uncomfortable at the thought of losing the old man, but happy at the thought of achieving a merchant's status. "I trust you will share it all with your younger brother and that young lady of yours? Maybe start a family soon?" the old man said with a wink. I could feel Titus starting to blush. He and the old man have a strong relationship, almost like father and son, but it made him uncomfortable to discuss his love life. Welcome to the club, Titus.

"You won't be going anywhere for a long time, Demetrius. Albus and I still have too much to learn from you."

"The only thing you two need to know is how to take care of your families. They are the most important things in this life. All the money in the world cannot buy that, trust me, I know. The Gods bless us with children so we may pass on our lineage to them. Though I never had children by blood, the Gods blessed me with you and Albus and I must make sure you will pass this on to your children. Otherwise, this was all for not," Demetrius said with a sigh.

"I promise, Demetrius. Your work will not be forgotten."

"It's not my work I care about, Titus. It's yours and your brother's."

I notice a frantic hand waving me down from the archway of the small store. It belongs to a young man, no older than 18. His features are eerily similar to mine, but he is much smaller and thinner.

"Do you recognize who this man is in your present life?"

It's definitely Darrin, but in this life he is my younger brother, Albus.

"Titus! I need some help over here!"

"I better go help him out. The high season is here and the Gods are smiling on us today, Demetrius!" Titus said, patting Demetrius on the shoulder.

"Yes, best he not drown in a sea of tourists."

The scene is changing. A woman is running toward me. I instinctively open my arms, enveloping her. She is shaking. I feel myself begin to laugh. She looks up at me, tears in her eyes. It's Liv.

"It's okay, Cassia, my love. Nothing is going to happen to this great city. Look at the wealth that is all around us! Certainly the Gods would not forsake us by dragging it to ruin. Look at the cloud," he said pointing to the dark mass in the distance. "It is so far away."

She nods her head in agreement. "You are right. The Gods would not erupt Vesuvius to destroy their most beautiful gift."

Vesuvius. Like Mount Vesuvius? As in the site of one of the worst eruptions in history, Vesuvius! I feel myself begin to panic and am forced out of Titus's physical body, now looking upon the scene.

"Where you are? What is the year?"

Pompeii, August 24, 79 A.D. The date appears clearly in my mind.

The scene changes again quickly. It's the same day, but looks to be hours later. The cloud is upon the city, billowing toward us at an increasing pace. I am watching my former self and Liv. Her eyes are not like they were in the other lives. The golden freckle is gone. Her eyes are colored a deep brown and wide like those of a child. People are running around, grabbing their jewels and clothing of intrinsic value. I feel like the center of the universe, still and stoic while everything else moves around me. Titus' mind can't catch up with what was happening.

My eyes fall onto Cassia. She is staring at Titus, her eyes bury into him willing him to come up with a solution. He just stands there, staring at the rolling black cloud. I feel a warm tear run down his face. Cassia grabs his arm, pulling me back into Titus's body.

"We have to run! The basement of the temple," she points to the largest building in sight. "Below the surface we can escape and pray to the Gods for protection." I can feel the initial blast of scolding debris against my arm.

"We have to get Albus and Demetrius. They are still in the market." We begin to run toward the storefront, but are stopped by a man wearing some sort of armor, a sword hanging from his side. He's extremely tall with a square face and stones for eyes.

"Is this man familiar to you?"

It is Billy Reid, rearing his ugly head once again.

"Where do you two think you are going? Trying to raid these merchants' shops while they run for their lives!" he said standing over me.

"No, no sir. I work for Demetrius Nero. We were going to help him to safety. You see, he is very …"

"Titus! Titus, come quick!" Albus screams from behind

the guard.

Titus storms past the gladiator and into the shop, Cassia following in his wake. Demetrius has fallen to the floor of the shop, trampled by a crowd running from the eruption billowing its way into the city. Albus races throughout the shop, trying to grab anything of value.

"Leave it," Demetrius said.

"What about your work? What about everything you wanted to leave behind!"

"My work means nothing if we are all dead. Leave everything."

Albus and I place Demetrius's arms over our shoulders and begin to run toward the temple. People pour into the basement one at a time. We are just behind the gladiator like guard, following him into the doorway, when he turns to face us.

"We only have enough supplies for three more. Leave the old man."

They all look at each other, silently electing Titus to speak. "Demetrius is a well-respected merchant of Pompeii. He will not be left to die in its rubble. I will share my rations with him," Titus said, stepping into the doorway.

The gladiator stopped me, blocking the entrance with his enormous frame. "I said only three. So you can bring in three or none at all. Your choice." Titus went silent, trying to think of a plan to save them all.

"Leave me," Demetrius said weakly. "I am frail. It is my time to meet the Gods. You three are too young for such a fate," he said, eyeing the gladiator. "Please, take them in."

"We aren't leaving you out here to die," Titus said, attempting to push his way into the temple.

"You stupid boy," the gladiator said laughing, raising his fist.

Before he could release his blow, Albus flew into the gladiator, catching him off guard and tackling him to the ground. "Albus, no!" Demetrius screams, freeing himself from Cassia's brace, using his last efforts to help Albus. In one swift movement, the gladiator pinned Albus, his knee pressing down on Albus's neck, forcing a loud pop. Albus's eyes went still, a long breath leaving his chest. Demetrius falls to his knees beside Albus, exhausting the last bit of energy in him. A man with a bag full of what looked like dried herbs hurries to Albus and presses his ear to Albus's chest. He looks to be the local medicine man.

"He is with the Gods now," he said in a small, mournful voice.

"Well, it looks like there are only three of you now. Would you like to join us?" the gladiator said with a smirk.

"I would rather meet the fiery death of the Gods a thousand times than be sequestered with you," Titus says as he launches himself at the large man, but is pulled back by Cassia, Demetrius standing between them.

"I will not lose you both today," Demetrius says, slowly walking toward the door. Tears fill Titus's eyes, his face ablaze with rage.

"Suit yourself. More rations for us," the gladiator said. "Here, take your friend," he said, tossing Albus's lifeless body to the ground outside the shelter. "We don't want him stinking up the place." With that, he bolted the door shut.

Titus dropped to his knees beside Albus's body, cradling his brother's lifeless head in his arms. "I'm so sorry, Alby. I'm so sorry," Titus said softly, rocking his brother's body back and forth. I had never lost Darrin before, in a past life, I mean. I felt Titus's pain radiate to every corner my mind. It was unbearable to even think about Darrin not being in my life. I could feel the burning of smoke in Titus's lungs, but he refused to leave Albus.

A sharp gasp escapes Demetrius. Titus turns to see the dark cloud creeping closer. A fragile hand touches Titus's shoulder. "We must get Demetrius to safety, the cloud is getting closer," Cassia said, kneeling beside Albus's body. "The Gods have him now," she said, gingerly closing Albus's eyes. "They will take care of him, just as you did during his life." Cassia leans down and kisses Albus's forehead, whispering a prayer into his ear. She gently touches Titus's face, moving his eyes to meet hers. "We must go, my love."

Titus nods and touches his forehead to Albus's, silently repeating the prayer. He gently places Albus's head on the ground and crosses his hands over his chest respectfully, and kneels before the body.

"Where will we go? The other buildings are bolted shut. How will we survive?" Cassia asks.

"If we can't get below the cloud, perhaps we can get above it and wait for it to pass," Titus said, pointing to the top of the temple.

Cassia and Titus quickly hoist Demetrius onto their shoulders and begin to climb the stone staircase to the roof of the temple. Demetrius is weak, like he can't take in a satisfying breath. The light he held within him was starting to fade. His eyes darted to every direction trying to grasp his surroundings.

Finally, we reach the top of the temple, the highest point in the city. Titus gently lays Demetrius on the roof and peers over the ledge at the blackened city below. The eruption's debris had not yet reached us, but we only have minutes until its heat invades our city. The cloud looks to be coming in just below our feet.

Cassia turns to Titus and smiles, "We did it!" Her tears make small trails down her ash-covered face. She throws herself into my arms and hugs him so tightly I can feel her heartbeat against his. Titus pulls her head away from his shoulder and stares into her eyes. They are perfectly still in a city melting away beneath their feet. He wipes the tears from her cheeks and kisses her. The black cloud is just below them now. Flecks of fire begin to appear within the black.

"Titus ..." I hear a small voice say. Immediately, he rushes to Demetrius. "Titus, it's time," he said, choking on his own breath. Demetrius takes Titus's hand in his own. "Take care of her," he said, squeezing his hand with all the might Demetrius had left inside him. "I love you, Son." Titus holds his hand as Demetrius exhales one last time.

"I love you too, Father," he whispers quietly. Solemnly, he places Demetrius's body into the same position as he left Albus and kneels before him in prayer. Cassia follows in suit. Slowly, Titus stands and looks down at Demetrius. "He was the only father I ever knew. He freed Albus and me from our chains, took us into his home, clothed us and taught us his trade. You and I would have never met had he not taken me into his care. To this day, I still don't know why he gave us such niceties."

"He has told you why all along," Cassia said. "For family." Titus's eyes don't leave Demetrius's body. "May I have a moment with him?" he asks Cassia softly.

"Of course, my love," Cassia said, heading toward the roof's ledge to view the ruin below.

Titus sits beside Demetrius's body silently staring at him. Even his mind is quiet despite the roar of the wind below him. I look over to Cassia to see her standing on the ledge of the roof, entranced by the circus below.

After a few moments, Titus turns to join Cassia. "At least we have each other, my love. We can build a new life when this settles," Titus said with a weak smile. Cassia smiles, kissing him lightly, their hands intertwined.

The wind below was picking up, whipping through the city like a tornado. Cassia turns to walk away from the edge, but she is met with a strong gust of wind, propelling her body over the edge of the temple. Titus holds on to her as she swings from the ledge, their hands still intertwined, fighting the wind to pull her to safety. Half of her body was already swirling in the fiery black cloud below, the force of it pulling Titus with her. I can feel her slipping through Titus's hand, the wind wiggling its way between our grasp. The smell of the flesh burning off of her legs fills my mind as the black wind surrounds her. His mind is racing. He would sooner be pulled in with her than let her go. Her face is screaming in pain.

Then, those words. She shouted those words. "Find me!" I feel her hand slip from Titus's and I am forced out of his mind and onto the roof beside him. Her body disappears into the cloud of burning ash and lava below. For a moment, his mind is quiet, unable to catch up with the present. He just stares into the empty space below where her body once hung. He knew he would not survive this. Maybe he would survive the travesty of Pompeii, but he would never survive losing his family. He drops to his knees and looks down into the cloud. "I'll find you, Cassia," he said. With that, he lets his body go limp and plunges into the cloud below. His screams ring through my ears as the burning ash scores his flesh. Quickly, his cries are silenced and Titus is lost.

For a moment, all I can hear is the wind. There is no one left to listen to.

"Awful, isn't it," a voice says from behind me.

It's Titus, but this time I wasn't surprised to see him.

"It could have been avoided, had I listened to her. It is now, and will always be, my greatest failure. I let my lust for money, for status, for a new life, cloud my judgment. We would all still be alive had I not insisted we stay to keep the shop open. Customer after customer complimenting my work, my family's legacy. Showering me with more riches than I thought I would see in my lifetime, but none of that matters without a family to share it with. Money is just currency – metal and paper. It comes and goes throughout your life, but you only have one family." I nodded, taking in each word.

"This was the start of it, you know."

"The start of what?" I questioned.

"The start of the loss. The start of the mistakes … yours and hers."

"But my father said we have lived over 60 lives together. Was this the start of all of our lives?"

"No, this was only the start of the mistakes that you did not allow the soul to rectify in your future forms. You made mistakes in your previous lives too, in the lives you have not seen. In your future physical forms, you were always able to learn from them as most souls do, but not this one. Time and time again you placed money, status, ignorance or stubborn pride before each other, and time and time again you lose each other. You have been given a rare gift, Nathan. Your insight into the past can aid in fixing your problems now. Not everyone is given that luxury, but I suppose someone is tired of seeing history repeat itself. You are very blessed."

"I'm starting to see that, Titus." Finally, for the first time in years, I felt a sense of clarity. "I think I am ready to go back now."

"You can go back any time, Nathan. All you need is a little push."

"What kind of pu..." But before I could finish my thought, Titus had pushed me over the roof's ledge and I was plunged into the black.

As I floated through the black, I saw my apartment in the distance. Dr. Rose was still sitting on my old couch, talking me back to the present. Just as I start to walk back into my apartment, something pulls me back. I turn and am greeted by a bright white light, not the kind that they talk about when you die, but the kind that heals you. I could feel it streaming through me, filling the empty holes inside me. There was a figure in the distance. I couldn't see a face or make out a gender, but it seemed nice enough. It started to speak, but the words flowed through my mouth. It was a message intended solely for Dr. Rose and myself. I could feel my mouth forming the words as my vocal chords released the sound. The voice was different from my own; it was low and ominous, but comforting.

"Grief finds its home in the bones of the soul, a festering wound each physical form must bear. It is a necessary poison to which there is no antidote. We place our soul in the hands of others lifetime after lifetime, and in return we all must experience a loss of the gift of our soul's bonds with others. This is the constant check and balance we must pay between this world and the next. The soul is a slow learner in that respect. After death, each soul is allowed to heal; it is what Nathan is feeling right now. But only in the physical state can the soul learn from the mistakes of past selves. To achieve inner peace is a slow burden.

"In the physical form, we have trouble accepting that death is not the end. The grief of loss causes many souls to live recklessly, numb themselves to the physical world, or simply cease to live. This is the wrong approach to grief. It deserves to be felt, but must be released. Grief is not meant to destroy you, but to enlighten you, to make you stronger. Grief should not hold the soul back from living, but instead give it new purpose. Using grief for good heals the soul and pays tribute to the bonds between souls."

The voice fell silent and the figure vanished. Instantly I fell back into my body, opening my eyes to a new present.

CHAPTER EIGHTEEN
Clarity

Dr. Rose and I sat in silence when I woke. For once, my mind was not racing. I had no questions, no qualms with what I saw. I felt enlightened, like I had found that piece of me that I locked away after my father died – the piece I pushed down so deep I'd hoped no one would ever make me face it. It was the piece I needed to keep living.

"Well, I don't know where to start with that," I said, attempting to break the silence.

Dr. Rose sat quiet, her mind trying to string the right words together before she spoke. "You are very blessed, Nathan. The bonds you have formed throughout your lifetimes are unbreakable, as was evident in this last regression. I have never had the pleasure of a master spirit speaking though a patient before. There must be something very special about you, about your purpose here."

"Is that what that was? That was really crazy. I was talking, but they weren't my words, but I could see it all happening, like I was watching myself though a window.

Why do you think they picked me?"

Dr. Rose took a long pause, reflecting on my question. "I think they picked you for the same reason you are here. You were lost and it is important to the balance of souls that you be found. Soulmates are a very real thing, Mr. James. They aren't always lovers as implied in fairytales; sometimes they aren't even friends. Their connection goes deeper than anything we can label. Plato described soulmates as once being one person, with two heads, four arms and four legs. But the gods were jealous of their happiness so they sent a lightning bolt down into each soul, splitting it in two and banishing them to opposite ends of the world, forced to spend eternity trying to find each other again. You have been lucky enough to find your soulmates throughout many lifetimes, and now you need to hold on to them. The masters seem to deem you worthy enough to receive this guidance from them directly. Don't squander their wisdom."

"Thanks, Doc. Not just for this, but for everything. I'm surprised that I didn't see you in these lives though? I feel like I would have seen you."

Dr. Rose chuckled. "Nathan, you didn't see me because it wasn't important to your journey. But I was there."

"What do you mean you were there?"

"After you told me about your first regression, I went back through the journals I kept on my own regressions. Each one of the lives you described matched up with one of mine, aside from your most recent lifetime during the civil rights movement. You did not recognize me, but I was there. I was the doctor that amputated your leg in the Civil War, I was the priest that laid Elisabeth to rest, which you did not see in your life as Brandt, and I was the medicine man that declared your brother dead in Pompeii. All of that was unimportant to your journey now. My purpose was to heal. I had failed you in my previous lives. Today, I was given another chance to rectify my mistakes. I fulfilled my purpose today." I could see the relief pour into her face, her stanch posture relaxed. A weight had been lifted from her, too.

"Well, should I come back for another regression? Is there still more for me to learn?"

"There is still plenty for you to learn, Mr. James, but perhaps it's time now to look toward the future instead of dissecting the past."

"Right again, Doc, right again. Well, I guess this is goodbye then?"

"No, Mr. James. This is 'See you soon'," Dr. Rose said with a smile.

"Right. Well, see you soon, Dr. Rose," I said with a smile, extending my hand.

"Cecilia," she said, ignoring my hand and embracing me.

"Right. See you soon, Cecilia," I said showing her to the door.

Just as she was about to leave she paused.

"Don't do anything tonight. Allow yourself to reflect on what you've learned. Your emotions have been put through the metaphorical ringer today. Take the evening to reflect. The answers will come to you. Act tomorrow."

"Will do. Get home safely."

"Do stay in touch, Mr. James. I am eager to see the great things that await you." With a wave and a familiar knowing smile, she disappeared down the staircase.

The apartment was quiet for the first time since I moved there. Even when we sat alone in our own worlds, Liv would fill the space with so much life. Even when it was quiet, the silent space felt alive. Now it was just me and my thoughts and for the first time, that didn't scare me. I grabbed my laptop and crawled into bed in an attempt to calm my thoughts.

After all that has happened, I had the urge to look up Billy Reid on social media to see where his life had gone. After scrolling through all the Billy Reids in the Virginia area, I came across a familiar face. His profile picture featured him with a beautiful woman and two small children. All of them were wearing matching sweaters and smiles a mile wide. I clicked on the picture to view his page, expecting that happy photo to be some kind of cruel mime, but to my surprise, Billy looked like a pretty great guy. All of his posts were family related, the most recent one being, "Celebrating our beautiful blessing! Happy 9th Birthday, Janey!" I scrolled through his pictures and found out that Billy had become a missionary. His wall was papered with photos of him building schools in Africa, working in local soup kitchens, even preaching a sermon.

Truth is, Billy made me feel like a real loser for the second time in my life. Billy built an entire school for children who would not have the privilege of education otherwise; he had a positive effect on the lives of innumerable strangers, and turned his life into something meaningful when he could have easily kept with his pattern of terror. He chose to give himself another chance.

I felt myself slipping back into the negative until I

remembered what Jackson had said to me at the beginning of this: "We are all individuals within one soul, operating for the same purpose." Billy learned his lesson and became the man he was supposed to be; he found his purpose.

I dug out my sketchbook from underneath my bed and dusted it off. Pencil in hand, I began to draw with no indication of what was going to come out. All the creativity I was scared to embrace, that I locked away inside of me when life got hard, invaded me all at once. My hands couldn't keep up with what my mind was thinking.

When I looked up, five hours and 52 pages had passed. I didn't see an old master's painting or edgy gallery piece. I saw a story. Blocks of sequential drawings filled each page. As I flipped back through the pages, it hit me. It's a comic book and we are the characters. They were all there, Brandt and Elisabeth, Jackson and Nelson, even Darrin and me as kids fighting the monstrous Billy. It was all there, everything that made us soulmates.

CHAPTER NINETEEN
Damage

The next morning, I woke up at 10 a.m., which was much earlier than I had planned on waking up considering I had finally hit the sack at around 5 a.m. Instinctively I searched for my phone, only to remember that it was making an epic voyage down the Hudson River. Because we live in the 21st century don't have a landline, it was time to do things the old school way, just like when Darrin and I were kids. I pulled on my ratty jeans and my chucks and bolted out the door.

Fifteen minutes later, I was standing in front of Darrin's apartment, sweating like a hog. The sun was beating down on the city that day, reflecting off of every glass surface turning the city into a concrete oven. Sweat dripped down my neck creating small pools near my collarbone. I couldn't tell if this was nerves or just the heat, but either way it was time to face the music. I pressed the button for 5B and waited for a familiar voice. No one answered. I pressed it again. Still nothing. Then I held down the button for 10 whole seconds. Finally, a voice came on the speaker.

"Somebody better be dying because there is no reason to be ringin' my bell this early on my day off!"

"Yo D, it's me," I said, trying to sound nonchalant.

There was a short pause, then a sarcastic tone. "Me? Me who? This voice sounds like my best friend Nate, but it can't be him, the guy who ran away and didn't tell anyone. Because anyone that hasn't called his best friend in three days must have a really good reason for it, like he was injured in a parasailing accident or was kidnapped and taken to a place with no phones."

"D, come on, I have to talk to you about some stuff. Seriously, dude I'm sorry. I'm an asshole."

A long static pause echoed on the other end of the speaker. "Do the song," he said finally.

"What? What song?"

"Nate, you know damn well what song I'm talkin' about. Do the song and I will know you're sorry. The moves, too. WITH the girly voice. I'm watching you on the camera."

"Come on, D, let me in. It's hot as balls out here! I'll do the song inside."

"Nope! Do it right there on the step and then you can come up."

"FINE!" I said, frustrated by my deserving punishment. I stepped back and waved at the camera. I cleared my throat, and began to shake my hips in arguably the most uncoordinated way possible and started to sing:

"*OH MY GOD BECKY, LOOK AT HER BUTT! IT IS SOOOOO BIG! It's like she's some rap guy's girlfriend or something. I mean it's just so ROUND and big. I mean, she's just so BLACK! I like big butts and I cannot lie, you other brothers can't deny, that when a girl walks in with an itty bitty waist and that round thing in your face, you get sprung! Wanna pull up tough …"*

"Fine, fine, you can come up. I'm not going to expose my neighbors to anymore of your dance moves. It's just sad at this point." I hear a long buzz releasing the door lock and bolt up the five flights of stairs to his apartment. By the time I reach the top, I am completely out of breath. Darrin is already standing in the doorway waiting for me. "How is it that we have been friends for, like, a million years and you still don't have rhythm? Seriously dude, it's embarrassing," Darrin says, teasing me.

"Yeah well, my best friend always shows me up when we go out, so I leave the dancing to him."

"Best friend, huh? Who is that? From where I'm standin' I'm just some dude that kinda knows you, who you can just run out on without so much as a 'see ya later'."

Darrin was mad and he had a right to be. I betrayed him, but I was going to make this right, even if it meant torturous embarrassment. "Darrin, I know I have a shitload of explaining to do, but more than that, I just want to say I'm sorry. I'm sorry I ran away. I'm sorry I've been a selfish dick. I'm sorry I wasn't there for you when Dad died. I'm sorry I left you to deal with everything on your own. You have always had my back, even when I didn't deserve it, but it never occurred to me that you needed the same. I have a lot to tell you about the past few days, but all that can wait. I just need you to know that I'm sorry, and … well … I love you, man."

My words didn't come out as eloquently as I had planned on the run over here, but judging by the look on Darrin's face, I had his attention. He stood there a moment, with a serious look on his face, processing my apology. That seriousness soon melted into a snarky grin.

"Dude, no homo, right? I mean, if you are figuring out your true self right now, that's totally cool! I can totally be your wing man, but I'm kinda super into the ladies right now," he said laughing. "Come here, man," he said with a one-armed hug. "You did seriously have me worried, though. I was at the police station filing a missing person's report when Liv called to tell me you were okay. It scared me, man."

"I know, that was really messed up of me. I don't even have an excuse for it, nothing that would make sense anyway."

"You want something to drink? Or maybe a towel?" he said eyeing my sweat soaked hair.

"Yeah, both would be great. So, uh, have you talked to Liv?" I tried to say as casually as possible, but Darrin saw right through my veiled attempt.

"You messed up, Nate. Like huge. I haven't talked to her since yesterday, but she was a mess. I think she took off from work all week."

As if I didn't feel like a complete asshole already. "Yeah, I know," I said shamefully.

"You're gonna fix it though. I've never seen two people so miserable without each other. That tells me you better do something pretty big. Let's start plannin'." He sat down on the couch beside me with two beers and a towel. Despite the fact that it was closing in on 11 a.m., I really needed that beer.

"Wait, before we get into that, don't you want to hear what happened? I want to explain why I left, I just want you to know …"

"It doesn't matter, Nate," he said, cutting me off. "You're my best friend and you're obviously going through some shit. I'm just glad you're okay. The reasons are just semantics. Whatever it was, you needed to do it so you could come back and shake your ass to our old talent show song as an apology and believe me, it was so worth it!"

"Remember the look on Mrs. Jones's face when "Baby Got Back" came on and I came out in that dress with a pillow strapped to my ass?"

"Yeah, we got through about the first chorus before she came out waving her hands, 'It was supposed to be The Backstreet Boys! THE BACKSTREET BOYS!' I think I saw a blood vessel pop in her forehead!"

"Remember what Dad said after?"

Darrin started cracking up, " 'The price we pay for superior art is pissing off the man!' Then he took us out for what we thought was going to be a beer."

" 'Beers all around! Heavy on the root for these two.' "

"He was awesome, man. Always knew how to make us feel better."

"Yeah, he really did." Darrin and I had never really talked about my dad before. We would occasionally bring up old memories, but never anything serious. I could see how much he missed him. It was written all over his face. Darrin always hid behind this funny guy act, but today he was transparent.

"Seriously though, you're okay, right?" Darrin said steering the conversation back toward the present.

That question had been the crux of my life for the past few days, and finally I could say, "I'm good. I'm really, really good," and mean it.

"Alright, well let's get plannin'. Have you thought about

anything you wanna do for her? I mean, this has to be kind of huge, like a proposal on 'Dancing with the Stars huge.'"

"Well, I'm not proposing, because I doubt she would say yes right now."

"But you're going to, right? I mean, don't take this the wrong way, but she is way out of your league. You need to lock that down."

"Well, yeah I'm going to do it, just not today. She needs something more than a proposal today. Here's what I was thinking." Darrin and I spent the next three hours drinking beers, laughing, and devising the perfect plan to win Liv back.

"Okay, so you have your part down?" I asked Darrin.

"Please, I invented the art of the win back. I got this."

"Alright, man," I said, heading toward the door. "See you on the other side!" Before I could make myself leave, I had to settle something, something that had plagued me for years, but didn't occur to me to ask until this moment.

"Darrin," I said turning back toward him, "why did you take that punch from Billy for me all those years ago when we were kids? I mean, you didn't know me from Adam and you just took a punch for me."

Darrin's permanent smirk slipped from his face and his tone became serious. "I guess … I guess I don't really know. I felt like I knew you were my friend even before I knew you. I don't know why, but I cared about what happened to you. Like we were supposed to be friends and that was the messed up ice breaker that brought us together."

I struggled to contain my smile. We were supposed to be friends, because we had been friends for centuries. I thought about telling him about our history, how he had saved my life, how we had always been there for each other. But in some inexplicable way, I think he already knew.

"Thanks, man. Just for the record, I would have taken that punch for you, too."

"Easy for you to say now!" he laughed. "Call me after and tell me how it goes. If it goes south, we will go for pity-party shots. If it goes well, we will go for celebration shots."

"Deal. Oh, also, did you know Billy grew up to be a missionary? Weird, right?"

"No way! I thought he would have been in a maximum security prison right now! I mean, he was crazy for a hot minute in school."

"Well, now he is married with kids and saving the world, apparently."

"Good for Billy. If more people turned their lives around like that, the world would be a much better place."

"Truth. Alright, I'm out. Thanks again, man."

"If she punches you, I will try to get there in time to move into the line of fire!"

On the way back to my place, I dropped by my cell carrier to grab a new phone and reconnect with the outside world. As nice as it was not having to deal with a cellphone pinging with mass texts and email chains, I was ready to rejoin reality. Also, I figured I should give my mom a call and let her know I'm alive.

"Hey, Kiddo! You back home safe and sound?"

"Yeah, got home late last night. I stopped by the farm on the way back."

"Why?" she asked, confused. "You haven't been back there for years. I can't believe you remembered how to get there!"

"I don't really know why, but something happened there I felt I needed to tell you about. I saw dad." For the next few minutes, I filled my mom in on my journey up the staircase. When I finished, the other end of the line was silent.

"Mom? Are you there?"

"Nathan, I'm only going to ask this once. Are you on drugs, Son? Because I will beat the ever living …"

"No! No, mom. I swear, I'm not on drugs. This really happened."

"Really, Nathan? I lived in the '60s and this sounds more familiar than I am willing to let on."

"Mom, I know this sounds insane, but I swear it's real." She went silent again.

"Did he ask about me?" she asked softly, scared of the thought that it might be real. I started to laugh, remembering what my dad asked me to tell her.

"He said that he definitely *did* fix the back wheel. I don't have any clue what that means though, do you?" I could hear her starting to cry and laugh simultaneously on the other end of the phone.

"I know exactly what it means." I could hear a smile in her voice.

"Well, could you fill me in? Because, quite frankly, I was expecting him to say something a little more lovey-dovey."

"When your father and I left Alabama to come back for New York after Nate and Belle died, we started fighting a lot. Neither of us would talk about what happened, so we took our grief out on each other. We wouldn't even

168

mention Nate and Belle. It was like when they died, we erased them from our memories so we didn't have to feel anything.

"That following Christmas, your father and I were driving to the farm to visit his parents for the holiday. Our back tire blew out and your father got out in the snow to put on the spare. It took all of 10 minutes before we were back on the road, but we yelled, blaming each other the entire time for something neither of us could have foreseen happening. After he supposedly 'fixed' the tire, we felt our car drop to the side again. Your father was furious at this point, so he got out to check the tire and the whole thing, rim and all, just fell off and started rolling down the road. Now, typically a tire would just roll a few feet and fall over, but not this one. I swear, both of us chased this rolling tire for a quarter mile down a dark back road until your father got close enough and literally tackled the rolling tire. He then picked up the tire, dropped to his knees and held it over his head victoriously.

"That was the first time we had laughed in months, it was the first time we told each other we were sorry for not being there for one another, and it was the first time we started to talk about Nate and Belle since they died. It was also the last time your father was ever allowed to work on any motor vehicle. That was a big turning point for us. We finally realized that to get through this, we needed to embrace each other, not push each other away. Maybe something you can learn from in your relationship …" she said, trying to turn the subject toward my current disaster. "Speaking of your relationship, how is Liv?"

"Subtle, Mom. Real subtle."

"I'm just saying, you better fix that, Nate. And how is

my Darrin? He called me after you left looking for you. He was worried sick, poor thing. You best be on your way to fixin' that one too. Just because he's family, doesn't mean you can trample all over his feelings and expect him to forgive you with open arms."

"D and I talked; we're good. As for Liv, I have a plan, but I don't want to jinx it by telling you. I think it will all be okay though."

"I'm sure it will be. You two make a great pair." She paused a moment. "Did your Dad say anything else?"

"Yeah, Mom. He said he loves you and he misses us. He hears you when you talk to him. It makes him feel good to know that you still like to ask his opinion on big decisions."

She was quiet a moment, but I could hear her smiling. "Thanks, Kiddo. That really made my day. Now go get that girl. Let me know how it goes!"

"Thanks, Mom. Love you."

"Love you too, Nate."

CHAPTER TWENTY

Metropolitan Museum of Art, Present Day

Even with the air conditioning on full blast, I am still sweating through my button-down shirt. Whether it's the heat or my nerves, it's not creating a great visual for why Liv would want to take me back. I quickly removed the sweat-stained shirt and put on an almost identical one in a different color. Usually, I reserve button-downs exclusively for work, but since I am jobless and trying to impress the girl I love, I thought it would be wise to make an exception. I texted Darrin to make sure our plan was going off without a hitch.

ME: We all set?

DARRIN: Operation Save Your Relationship has commenced. Be there at 7 p.m. sharp and don't look like crap. Good luck.

Darrin had played his part perfectly. He called Liv after I left his apartment and asked to meet up with her on the roof of the Met for a drink, to see how she was doing. This might seem weird to most people, considering Darrin is *my* best friend, but he and Liv had become great friends over the years. Everything was falling into place; the rest was up to me.

I grabbed the messenger bag Liv bought me last Christmas, hoping to score some extra points with her, and left for the Met. My nerves started to creep into my thoughts as I walked. I was excited, but terrified. I missed Liv. It felt like it had been weeks since I saw her last.

In the corner of my eye, I spotted the most beautiful sunflowers outside of a bodega on the corner of 91st and 3rd. On our first real date, I brought Liv a single sunflower because, at the time, it was all I could afford in addition to the dinner I bought on Groupon. I didn't know it at the time, but it was her favorite flower. She said that's how she knew I was "someone worth keeping around." I purchased the largest, brightest one from the bunch.

Sunflower in hand, I started up the giant steps of the Metropolitan Museum of Art with a newfound confidence. When I left my apartment, I had no idea what I was going to say; I was just going to wing it. But I ascended the tall steps, the words poured forth like they had been there all along.

My heart was thumping against my chest as the elevator doors opened to the rooftop garden. Navigating the giant balloon animal statues, I finally spotted a familiar shape. There she was, standing at the opposite end of the roof staring down at Central Park, her back to me. The sun was setting, illuminating the specks of red in Liv's blond hair. I stood there, just for a moment, and took in the view. The tall buildings were just a black shadow against the painted sky.

Okay, Nate, you can do this. Just walk up to her. Just walk up to her and tell her what's in your head. I took a deep breath and started toward her.

"Sorry I'm late."

She barely turned her head. "You're about three days late." The sting in her voice had grown harsher. When she left the other night, she was almost weak. Now she just sounded angry. "Let me guess – Darrin isn't really coming."

"No, no it's just me," I responded.

"Alright," she said turning to face me. "Well let's hear it, Nate. What did you come here to say? What's the grand explanation that's supposed to make all of this magically go back to normal?" Her eyes were solid, locked on mine. Her mouth was pressed into a thin line. "Well, come on! What did you come here to say? Did you come here to apologize for walking out on the people you claim to love? Are you here to apologize for treating us like shit because you feel sorry for yourself? Please enlighten me, Nate!"

I couldn't move, I couldn't breathe. She was so angry it scared me. Before I could get a word out, she stormed past me, heading for the stairs down to the main floor. I couldn't let her leave, not again.

"Olivia, stop!" I shouted, inviting the eyes of everyone on the rooftop to follow my apology. She hesitated and then stopped at the door. I walked over to her, until her face was inches from mine. She wouldn't lift her gaze to meet mine. "Olivia, please give me a chance to make this right. Give me a chance to explain this." I gently touched her cheek, steering her eye toward mine, but she pushed my hand away. "Please, give me a chance." As I was begging, a thought occurred to me. What if she said no? What if this didn't work? I couldn't let that happen, not again.

"Actually, no, no I take that back. You will give me a chance," I demanded. She finally met my gaze with an angry, baffled look. "You will give me a chance because I love you. I love you and I know you love me and when you love a person, you open yourself up to them hurting you. That's the risk we run loving another person. I'm done hurting each other. I'm done waiting for that magical moment when I realize what I'm supposed to do with my life, because it doesn't matter. The job, my art, money, none of that matters without you. You are my future. You are what I am supposed to do with my life; the rest is just a blank to fill. I love you, Olivia. That's why you will give me another chance, because without you my life is not a life. It's just floating through time, waiting for you to come back. I finally found you and I'm not letting you go again."

I reached into my messenger bag and pulled out a small wooden frame. "I saw the past, and I didn't like it. It was painful, more painful than anything I have ever felt in this lifetime, but I have a chance to make that right now. When I look into my future, this is what I see."

After I left Darrin's, I'd rushed home to put our plan into action. I had something I needed to get out of me and on to paper. I had drawn my past already, but like Dr. Rose said, it was time for me to focus on my future.

"Is this us?" she asked, looking wearily at the drawing.

"Yeah, well my version of us when we are older. I learned how to age a subject in a criminal justice class in college. It's not perfect, but …"

"It's exquisite," she said, cutting me off.

"Really? You don't think it's creepy that I drew us as old

people sitting in your chair?"

"Surprisingly, no," she said softly. "It's actually everything I have ever wanted you to say to me, but never did. I just wanted to know that I was enough. That though the road might get bumpy, I would be enough to keep you steady. That's all I ever wanted from you." Her long face turned into a light smile.

"Why didn't you ever tell me that?"

She thought a moment, her eyes turned toward the ground like her mind was talking to her. "I knew … I know you love me, that was never the problem. You always had these amazing ambitions. That was one of the reasons I fell in love with you. Your passion was overwhelming and your attitude was so positive. It was contagious, like you knew that you were going to be something. It gave me hope. Then one day, you just faded. I watched you slowly giving up, accepting the way things were and fall into a comfortable coma of work you hated. You used excuse after excuse to justify not taking a risk on yourself. I knew that if you didn't try to go for your dreams, I would never be enough to fill that void for you. You can pursue your dreams forever and maybe you will make it, maybe you won't. But I want to be the constant in your life like you are in mine. I want to be your future, no matter how life turns out for us." She smiled, still looking at the drawing.

"You want to get out of here?"

"Yeah, I think we have made enough of a scene for tonight. So was this the big 'win her back gesture'? Is there a marching band waiting to play 'The Way You Look Tonight' we should wait for?"

When Darrin and I were planning this afternoon, he

asked me the same thing. "Seriously, dude? You're going to draw her a picture? Literally draw her a picture? You're doomed," he said. But I know Liv. She isn't the spectacle type. She can remember every time I ever brought her flowers, but not which birthday it was that I threw her a monster surprise party. She notices the details, the little things that tell her I love her. That's how I knew this would work.

"I have a few more things to show you, but yeah, this is the gesture."

"It's perfect." She kissed me for what felt like the first time. I wrapped my arms around her like she might float away if I didn't hold her. Everything clicked into place, like the last piece of a puzzle.

"Let's go home."

CHAPTER TWENTY-ONE
Beginning

After Liv and I left the Met that night, I told her everything. I told her about Jackson, Brandt, Nate, Titus, even seeing my dad. I was an open book to her for the first time in our relationship. It was cleansing. I felt a weight lift from us. She listened quietly, her mind working through each story. I talked for what felt like for hours, explaining every last detail of what I saw. When I finally finished, she was silent but I could see questions forming in her mind.

"So after all this, what do you believe?" I realized I hadn't stopped to reevaluate what my new beliefs entailed.

"I don't know what I believe, but I do know I believe in something. There has to be something more out there. This can't just be sheer fiction. I'm intrigued. I want to learn more about other beliefs and how they relate to what I have seen. What do you believe after all this?"

"Well," she said gathering her thoughts, "I believe what I have always believed. I believe there is something bigger than us that we won't understand until we need to. I place my faith in the universe and its plan for me. I believe the lives that you saw are real. I also believe in you, in your abilities and your passions. You have just grazed the surface of what you can accomplish."

Just then, I remembered the comic book I drew the previous night. "I kind of started on something, after I saw Dr. Rose last night." I handed Liv the sketchbook. "I didn't even know what I was drawing, like someone else was guiding my hand. All of this just started to flow out at once. I have ideas for more, but this is just a start. What do you think?"

She was quiet, absorbing each page. "It's beautiful, Nate. Unexpected, but really beautiful. It is so reflective of you. I feel like in the past when you painted, you were so focused on getting every detail right that the work lost its essence, but this is so … free." She flipped to the page about Darrin and I and started to chuckle. The drawing reflected the infamous battle with Billy Reid. I drew Darrin wearing a cape, puffing out his chest with his right hand raised to Billy and me peeking out from behind his shoulder. Billy is giant and green, almost Hulk-like, his fist reared behind his head.

"Have you shown him this? He would love looking like a superhero."

"I think he would like it a little too much. I haven't shown it to him yet, but I will. I wanted you to be the first to see it."

She gave me a coy look and returned to the sketchbook. "So what's next? What do you think you will do with it?"

Honestly, I hadn't thought that far ahead. I was so focused on getting Liv back that I didn't really care what came next. "I don't know. Maybe make it into a comic book or something?"

"I think it's more of a graphic novel. You have enough material here for a few of them. Why don't you send some out and see if you get a response? I think this could be really ..."

"Right now, I just want to be with you. I don't want to think about tomorrow or next week or next month. I just want to be here, right now, with you," I said slipping beside her, wrapping her in my arms.

"I'd like that too," she said. She kissed me lightly. "Thank you for coming to find me. Part of me thought you might just let me go because it was easier."

"I could never do that," I said lifting her into my lap. I held her face in my hands, pressing her forehead to mine. I tried to restrain myself, but I couldn't hold myself back any longer. I pulled her lips to mine and kissed her aggressively, pages of my drawings spilling into the floor.

She pulled herself on top of me in a straddle. Her fingers wound into my hair, stimulating every follicle. A fire spread through my chest and down my torso. I picked her up, her legs still wrapped around my waist, and gently laid her on our bed. I kissed her slowly, every piece of her. A symphony of moans and stolen breaths escaped her. Gooseflesh covered every inch of her body as my lips made their way down her stomach, my tongue tracing a path. I moved south. Her breath tightened, her nails lightly clawing at my shoulders. I grabbed her hands as I worked and pinned them to the mattress beneath us. I could feel her building, pulsating against my tongue, begging for release. A long cry escaped her, her limbs settling into the mattress in relief. I released her hands, running my fingertips along the soft skin of her thighs.

I pulled my lips to hers, kissing lightly down her neck,

her muscles relaxed in ecstasy. She reached a free hand below and pulled me inside of her, rolling me onto my back, stealing my position. The view of her above me is stunning. She was more beautiful in that moment than I had ever seen her. We shared something deeper now, we shared the same risk. I allowed her inside of me, to know me, and still she loved me, all of me.

My breath shortened into small wisps of air. I grabbed her hands, weaving her fingers with mine. I could feel her building too. We released together, exploding in relief. She collapsed onto my chest, both of us desperate for air, her chest rising and falling onto mine, skin-to-skin. I stroked her hair and kissed the top of her head, silently begging her not to let me go.

That night, Liv and I slept soundly, wrapped in each other. There were no dreams of death, no 2:36 a.m. wakeup call, no cold sweats. There was only peaceful sleep.

CHAPTER TWENTY-TWO
Aftermath

Turns out, Liv was right. My graphic novels were something awesome. I started putting words to the pictures and binding them into graphic novels. One blissfully unemployed day, I was at Starbucks tuned into the Zen Focus playlist on my Spotify, putting the final touches on Titus and Cassia, when I felt a tap on my shoulder. I must have looked startled because the man behind me backed away quickly as I turned around. He had salt and pepper hair with an equally speckled beard. He was slender and wore jeans and a blazer with a vintage Iron Man T-shirt underneath.

"Apologies, I didn't mean to startle you. What are you drawing?" he asked.

"Oh, I'm kind of trying to draw or ... write a series of graphic novels."

"Interesting," he said, intrigued. "You don't see many graphic novels taking place in Pompeii, but it does certainly set the scene for a graphic novel. May I?" he said, gesturing to my sketchbook.

"Uh, sure, but they aren't totally finished, so don't be too harsh on me." The man flipped through the most intimate stories of my lives, his face focused intently, clearly taken aback.

"These are quite impressive. How did you come up with this stuff?"

"Well, I was kind of there," I said unsure how to answer his question. The man laughed and handed the sketchbook back to me.

"Listen, I'm really intrigued by what you've got going on here and that doesn't happen often. This is different from anything I've seen." He pulled out a card from his pocket and handed it to me. "I work with comics, sci-fi and graphic novels. We are always looking for new original work, especially now with the explosion of graphic novels hitting mainstream media. Send me an email and we will set up a time for you to come into the office. I would really like to see more of your work. What was your name?"

"Nate … Nathan James," I stuttered.

"Nate, great to meet you. I hope I hear from you soon," he said, cheering me with his venti iced coffee before leaving the cafe.

Every person that has ever moved to New York City has heard a story about somebody who knew somebody who caught a big break. Being the skeptic I am, I knew better. Nobody catches breaks anymore. Except sometimes, people do catch breaks and this time, that somebody was me.

Richard England was the CEO of a mid-sized publishing house in Brooklyn. I met with him on August 22, exactly 10 years after I had planned to end my life, which was a little too poetic, even for me. On August 23, I received a contract from Richard for the publication of one graphic novel, with the promise of writing four more, providing an initial advance of $68,000 per novel, plus royalties and a clause for possible on-screen syndication.

I asked Richard later why he stopped me that day in the coffee shop. "I don't know, honestly. Your work actually wasn't the thing that stopped me, it was you. Your determination. How you took so much care of the figures you were drawing. I actually stood there and watched you draw for about five minutes before I started to feel like a stalker and decided to approach you. Who knows, maybe we knew each other in another life." At this point, nothing would surprise me.

When Richard found me, I was the poorest I had ever been. I spent that summer living on a weekly unemployment check of $367.50, drawing at various coffee shops during the day, meeting Darrin for $2 beer happy hours after his work day, and making a game out of finding the cheapest dates for Liv and me on weekends. It was the greatest summer of my life and I hadn't worried about my future once, because I knew I was right where I was supposed to be. Right here, with my soulmates.

Inspired by my determination, Liv decided to cut her hours at the restaurant and spent the majority of her time composing. She would spend hours inside her headphones creating these elaborate pieces. After contacting an old music professor at Juilliard, Liv got a gig playing a small concert at Lincoln Center as part of a graduate showcase. She spent a few weeks teaching her composition to a group of six musicians, including herself on the cello. Liv decided to not let me hear the piece she was working on until it was absolutely perfect.

The night of the concert, she brought the house down. I came in expecting a Beethoven-style concerto piece, but it was so much more. She mixed a classical style with a heavy, almost hip-hop beat. It was like nothing I had ever heard before. Three professional musicians, all Juilliard alumni, sat in the audience that night and all three approached Liv after the show. She was a magnetic force that evening. People have always been drawn to her, but that night it was like she was the brightest burning star in the sky.

One of the women in attendance was the chairman of the board at the New York Philharmonic. She was particularly impressed by Liv's composition and asked to meet with her later that week to discuss her future. The woman was smitten with Liv's positive attitude and passion. Now Liv has a freelance contract with the Philharmonic to compose and, for some performances, play in concert on the cello.

Darrin is killing it at his job and loving every minute. Lately, he has even been filling in on ESPN College Football when an anchor is out. ESPN is talking about finding him a permanent segment on the show. His new position sent him traveling to different schools during the pre-season to interview new up-and-coming stars.

I think he envied the players at times. His first love was always football and when he didn't make it to the NFL after college, he took an internship at ESPN hoping to get noticed. Darrin is an incredible player, smarter than a lot of the guys on the highest paid pro teams, but for some reason he didn't make it. Maybe that just wasn't his path, I don't know. He seems happy to be in the action of it all, but deep down I know he misses being on the field.

I'm still adjusting to the fact that being a famous artist isn't in my future. After my advance came through, my daily life didn't change much. I still spent the same amount of money I usually did, save for one very expensive gift, and I still worked on my novels. Richard believed in my work so much that he devoted a large portion of their marketing budget to my novels, which paid off tremendously. The novels were PG enough that parents would buy them for their kids, but intriguing enough to attract an older audience. I was asked to do book signings, even a press tour once things really started to pick up.

As I stitched together each past life depiction with words, I couldn't help but wonder if there were records on these various people. They had been so real in my visions. I had their names, where they lived, even sometimes the years that they lived. One by one I explored each time period, hunting for any evidence of my previous existence. To my surprise, I found quite a bit of information on my former selves.

Jackson Holdsworth was a prominent blacksmith in the Petersburg area of Virginia until he was drafted to the Civil War. I even found a photograph of the old tintype of Jackson with his wife and child, just like the one in Lucy's locket. I read that he had shot and killed 352 men during the Civil War, a record for a Confederate soldier. He was even awarded a medal after his death by General Lee prior to the South's surrender.

King Brandt was very interesting. Though he only ruled a small kingdom for a very short amount of time, he was written about in numerous historical texts. "Brandt the Mad" they dubbed him, calling out his insane conversations with inanimate objects, his refusal to rule his subjects and his abundant drinking problem. His insanity seemed to overshadow even his bride. Though Queen Elisabeth was written about fondly, her name faded from the texts when it came to the charge she lead, and died in, to save her kingdom. She was merely a footnote in that pivotal moment.

Though I had found out so much about my former selves, it still plagued me that I couldn't identify Belle and Nate's killer. For months I searched for evidence of a Chet, any Chet, at the University of Alabama and came up empty handed. Then one fateful morning when I was making breakfast, a familiar face popped up on the news.

"We have breaking news on the Chester J. Baxter, Jr. case. Chester 'Chet' Baxter, Jr. of Alabama's prominent Baxter & Sons, has admitted to the attempted murder of his business partner, Thomas Riddell. Baxter's confession came after a very controversial video surveillance tape was submitted into evidence by Riddell's lawyers, in which Mr. Baxter alludes to having 'killed your people before' and using specifics such as 'I was bashing heads of (expletive) like you before you were allowed to vote.'

"During the course of this four-month trial, several people have stepped forward to accuse Baxter of assault, including Baxter's now ex-wife, Maurine Baxter. To recap, upon hearing about the assault on Riddell, Mrs. Baxter submitted Mr. Baxter's collection of rare baseball bats into evidence to be tested for blood and damage consistent with the allegations, claiming this was his weapon of choice. Mr. Baxter was found by Mr. Riddell's secretary who entered the scene of the assault after hearing a heated argument coming from Mr. Riddell's office turn violent. 'Mr. Baxter was holding a baseball bat to Mr. Riddell's windpipe, attempting to strangle him,' states Riddell's secretary in previous testimony. We will continue to follow this case closely and update our viewers with more news as it breaks. Reporting from Birmingham, this is Charise Delacart."

As I stared into the face of my past self's killer, I felt closure. There was no justice for Nate and Belle, but it didn't hurt that the man was arrested for what could have turned into the same crime. I could think of a few other punishments better suited for his crimes, like getting eaten by an alligator or ripped to shreds by a great white after his yacht sank, leaving him stranded in dark water for hours, but this was fitting, too, I suppose.

For Titus, I found nothing. Not even a small mention of his existence in Pompeii. So I decided to do one extravagant thing with the money I received and find out something more about him. Liv and I planned a trip to southern Italy to visit Pompeii, the site where everything began.

As we toured Pompeii, my mind darted in every direction, unable to focus on just one relic. Everything was familiar. I knew where each street led without having walked it. Pompeii was exactly as I remembered it from my regression, only completely desiccated. Even through the unbearable heat of that summer day, Liv's hand was enclosed in mine.

"This was the largest temple in the city, the Temple of Jupiter. Jupiter was the highest of the Roman gods at this time, superseding the Greek god Apollo as Roman influence grew in Pompeii. Jupiter was known as the ruler of gods and the Protector of Rome ..." The tour guide's voice trailed as she kept moving to the next attraction. My feet were cemented to the ground, my body frozen.

"This is it, isn't it?" she asked. I could only nod. I couldn't speak. I couldn't breathe. It was real. I still had lingering doubts about the regression, unable to silence that skeptical piece of my mind, but there was nothing more real than what was standing right in front of me.

The tour group moved ahead, but we stayed behind to marvel at what once held the most important moments of our lives. Liv looked around, checking for the peering eyes of security guards. When the coast was clear she reached out and touched a column of the ruin. There was something so familiar about watching her fingers explore the crevices of the stone. I stared at it, trying to remember what it looked like in my regression. Liv ran ahead to catch up with the group, but I remained fixated on the temple, silently thanking God, the universe, whatever the hell it was that brought be back here to find myself.

A few moments later, I feel a light hand on my shoulder. "You have to see this, Nate. You are not going to believe it." Liv grabbed my hand and pulled me toward the tour guide. "Tell him what you just told me."

The woman gestured to the mummified bodies behind her, "You mean about the lovers?"

"Yes, he will find it very interesting."

"The two people you see behind me are a male and female we found about 10 meters from the Temple of Jupiter. The woman was found laying to the right of the man, who was positioned about six meters to her left. His arms, as you can see, are outspread toward her. As you can imagine, material items along with human remains were scattered everywhere when the disaster struck. We pride ourselves in trying to put the stories of this community back together through a number of clues - any fibers left on the body, shoe remnants, jewelry, anything that may link them to their life in Pompeii.

"These two were found pretty far apart, so we figured they were not in any way related, but then we found a similarity. Both bodies had the same traces of metal in their left hand, embedded in their ring fingers. The metal is very unique for the time, especially to be used in jewelry. It must have come from an old family sword; it was definitely handmade. Most of the metal jewelry we find here are your typical silver and gold, but this stood out. By the way the bodies were positioned and the metal fragments found on them, we concluded that they were married. That the man was trying to save his wife."

"Thank you," Liv kindly said to the woman. The guide nodded and moved on to gather her group. "It's us, Nate."

It was us. I took Liv's head in my hands and looked deep into her blue eyes. The golden fleck I had grown to love was reduced to nothing more than a small speck. I hugged her close, ignoring the sweltering heat.

"I was going to wait to do this somewhere amazing like the Trevi Fountain, but I don't think a moment can be more perfect than right now." I had been fingering my pocket all day, checking to make sure it was still there. I was sure she was onto me the second I suggested we take this trip, but apparently I kept it pretty low profile. My heart was beating so loudly I was sure she could hear it. A bead of sweat rolled down my cheek, a mix of heat and nerves. The lump in my throat made my voice drop at least three octaves. I removed a ring from my pocket that was so perfectly Liv. A large oval sapphire nestled perfectly into a vintage filigree setting.

Choosing the perfect ring was intimidating, so Darrin came with me to the small jewelry shop on 46th Street for moral support. The store had a million options - round, square, oval, white gold, platinum, yellow gold. It was dizzying. Darrin and I pored over diamond after diamond for hours, but nothing seemed right.

Then the clerk brought out an antique piece he bought at a recent estate sale. "Dude, that is so Liv," Darrin said as we inspected the ring. The deep blue of the sapphire reminded me of Liv's eyes at their happiest. I could see her wearing this every day for the rest of our lives. The cost was significantly more than the diamonds I had been looking at, but I knew this was the one.

I had been crafting my next question unintentionally since the day I met Liv. Somewhere inside of me, I always knew it was her. We shared something that no one else ever understood. With a deep breath, I dropped to one knee in front of the place where our journey to now began and recited the words I had been practicing in the mirror for months.

"Olivia Hammond, will you do me the great honor of spending the rest of eternity with me as my wife and my soulmate?" Her eyes said 'yes', but the words hadn't been spoken. She looked at me speechless and knelt to my level. I heard a small whisper escape her between gasps for air.

"What was that?" I asked jokingly.

She looked at me with a smile. "YES! Of course!" she said throwing her arms around my neck, squeezing me so tightly I was sure she could feel the beat of my nervous heart against her chest. We sat there silent, just soaking in the moment. No one had even noticed the proposal. It was a flash in the pan compared to our time together, but it felt like the picture had finally been completed.

CHAPTER TWENTY-THREE

New York City, Present Day

At one particular book signing, there had to be at least a hundred people there just to see me. It was surreal how fast word spread about my novels. They had gathered a healthy following by the time the fourth instillation was due to come out.

As I sat at the front of a tiny bookstore in Brooklyn signing copies of *Death and Resurrection: Volume 4*, the line seemed to grow. It took hours to sign each person's book, but I didn't mind. Finally, the very last three people stood in front of me, two young boys about nine years old, one black, one white, and a middle aged woman, presumably their mother. The kids were like child doppelgangers of Darrin and me, the way they were joking and shoving each other.

"That's enough, boys. It's our turn!" the woman said. "Say hi to Mr. James and thank him for signing your books."

"Thank you, Mr. James!" the boys said in unison.

"You are quite welcome. Thank you for reading my

book! I think you guys might be my youngest fans. Your mom must be extra cool. What are your names?"

"I'm Keith and this is Chris ... Christopher." Keith had a very short blond buzz cut with a large scar visible just above his left ear.

"Mr. James?" said Keith. "Are these stories real? I mean, do you think we really can live another life after this one?"

"I do believe that. I think we can live a lot of lives. What do you think?" I asked, turning to Christopher. His large brown eyes gazed down at his fidgeting hands.

"I hope so. I want to be able to see my best friend again. I'm gonna miss him after ..." his voice trailed off and I heard a sniffle in his voice. The mother leaned down to Christopher at eye level and spoke to him softly, not like a child, but like a caregiver.

"It's going to be okay. I know you're scared. I am, too, but remember what Jackson told us about best friends?"

"That best friends are more than that, they are more like brothers. They will always be together no matter what."

"That's right! You and Keith are best friends, so no matter what happens, you will see each other again. Why don't you two go check out your cool signed books while I talk with Mr. James a minute, okay?"

"Okay, mom! Don't forget to ..."

"I won't! Now go on, you two." The two boys raced each other over to children's fiction with their newest literary adventure.

"Mr. James, I just wanted to thank you for your book. You have helped our family tremendously," the mother said, handing me a small envelope.

"What's this?"

"It's a thank-you note from the boys. They asked me to give it to you because they were too shy."

"Well, you are most welcome! I've never gotten a thank-you letter from a fan before."

She sighed, casting her eyes downward. "Keith was diagnosed with a brain tumor, stage three, a few months ago. The doctor's took out the tumor, and they think they got it all, but only time will tell. It's been rough trying to explain the possibility of death to Keith and Christopher, more so to Christopher. Keith hasn't felt sick physically, so I don't think he fears dying, but Christopher is another story. His father died when he was very young, so it's just him and his mother now. He is so fearful of being left behind without Keith, just like when he lost his father. He started acting out at school and at home. He has seen the school guidance counselor, his mother and I have spoken with him, but nothing seemed to work until we found your novel.

"I know I will probably get the bad parent of the year award for letting them read such violent stories, but they actually focused on the moral of each story instead of the fighting. The boys loved the story about Jackson and Nelson and how they were really David and Ethan in present life. It gave them hope of seeing each other again. They have been different kids since then. They're happier, making good grades, acting like normal kids. I have even recommended it to other parents in the same situation. We are all really grateful to you for your book. It's touching a lot of lives," she said.

I was speechless. I looked over at the two boys, whispering and laughing. It was hard to believe that one of them was sick, let alone fatally ill. "I don't know what to say. I had no idea."

"You don't need to say anything. There are no words that can salve a wound like that; only things that can help you get through it, like your book. We just really wanted you to know how thankful we are." With a smile and a squeeze of my hand, she headed toward the two boys.

I didn't open the letter until I got home that night. I had never interacted with children before, not because I didn't want to, the opportunity just never presented itself. The letter was handwritten in near perfect 4th grade cursive.

Dear Mr. James,

It's us, Keith and Christopher. We are your biggest fans. You are the coolest, smartest guy ever. We really like the story about Jackson and Nelson. They are our favorite characters. Some of your stories are too lovey dovey, but that's okay, because Jackson and Nelson are cool.

We are best friends just like them. When Keith went into surgery to get his tumor out, I stayed with him the whole time until the stupid hospital people kicked me out, just like Nelson did with Jackson. Nelson and Jackson taught us that we can be strong and sad at the same time. We felt bad that Nelson was all alone when Jackson died, but when we found out that they got to be new guys in another life in the future, it made us feel better. The future is way cooler than the Civil War anyway, so they were lucky that they came back when we have TV and computers and stuff. Life without TV would suck (don't tell my mom I said that).

I think me and Keith are just like Jackson and Nelson. We are best buds forever and ever. If we ever die, before all the doctors invent something that keeps us alive forever, I think we would see each other again. Even if I was born in America and Keith was born in China,

I think we would still know each other.

So thanks for writing the book, Mr. James. I can't wait until you write more of them. I hope they make a movie out of them. That would be so awesome!

Sincerely,
Christopher and Keith

P.S: If you want us in your next book or in a movie, we are available. Here is my number- 646-555-3553. Just tell my mom you want to talk to me. We would be super cool as characters.

I have received a lot of fan mail since my novels started to take off. Some from women enamored with Liv and my love story, some from grown men looking for something more in life that they just can't seem to put their finger on, but mostly from people my age who felt so lost it was consuming their daily lives. I've gotten hate mail from super religious organizations damning me for believing in reincarnation and letters of admiration from high-ranking religious leaders praising me for my beliefs. But never have I received a thank-you letter from someone who understood what my stories were really about, let alone from two nine-year-old boys.

We all have a purpose in life. Some of us know what we are going to be from the time we are 3 - years -old. Some of us find out later. I thought I was going to be a fancy artist, paintings in the Met, the Louvre, everywhere, but that wasn't my journey. My journey was to give two young boys from Brooklyn hope of being friends beyond the prospect of death.

Those two boys gave me hope that I was following my intended path, but I still couldn't expel the lingering doubts that what I saw in the regressions was all a fabrication comprised of information I had collected over a lifetime, conveniently stitched together to resemble a story that would push me out of my creative rut. Though I had researched these people, I had no concrete evidence that I was them. I studied the Civil War and Pompeii in school, I could have learned about Brandt too; and perhaps I saw a photograph of Nate and Belle and pieced together their story when I was young, then simply forgot. The more I thought about the events of the past year, the more clouded my mind became. I needed hard evidence. Something tangible. Something indisputable.

Though I had my doubts about my past lives, I surrendered to my newfound belief in the afterlife. I can't explain what happened in my tree that day, but I am choosing to believe that my dad is looking out for me.

I decided to visit my dad for guidance. Not up the staircase, but his gravesite. I felt pulled there. I still don't believe he resides beneath the dirt, but it's nice to have a physical spot to visit him, rather than climbing a mythical staircase to carry on a conversation in my mind.

Liv had come home with me plenty of times, but she had never seen the farm where I spent my summers or the site where my father is buried. It was time to let her into that part of my life.

The cemetery is situated on three acres of land between two very distant crop fields. It seemed to sit alone, hidden on the side of a back road. When we drove up the gravel path to our family's plot, my stomach started to turn. The last time I was here was the day I buried my father.

I sat in the car staring at the tombstone. It seemed unrealistic that my father was buried there after all I had seen. Liv took my hand and together we stood six feet above a handful of ash that once was a part of my father.

"Do you want to talk to him?" Liv asked.

"No, I know he isn't there. I don't know why I felt the need to come here. After I met those two boys, I just wanted to feel close to him."

I leaned down to examine the tombstone. It's more worn than I remembered. I dusted the loose dirt off its polished surface. Burrowed in the grass, I noticed the reflection of something shiny. A small brass button was pressed into the ground, spreading the leaves of grass outward.

"Did you drop this?" I asked Liv, handing her the button.

"No, but this looks just like the one I bought from the thrift store. Maybe some Civil War veterans are buried here. Someone probably placed it on a near by grave in memorial. The wind must have blown it over here," she said, handing the button back to me.

I ran my thumb over the insignia. This wasn't a coincidence. Civil War buttons aren't just laying around in Southern graveyards. A few plots away, I spotted a pair of weathered gravestones. I approached them cautiously, but I knew who they belonged to.

Jackson Holdsworth, Corp. Co. B, 71st Reg. Mil. Virginia, 1841-1863 read the inscription on one. The words encircled the Confederate seal. *Could this be how I created Jackson? Had I seen this marker the day of my father's funeral and filed it away in my memory?*

I ran my fingers gently over the tattered letters, tracing

each line. My hands explored the edges of the jagged stone, looking for clues.

"Ouch!" I exclaimed, jerking my hand from its course. A sharp edge sliced the palm of my hand. Blood started pooling at the surface. My ears started to ring. I felt Liv cradling my wounded hand, but couldn't hear her speaking.

"I don't feel go…"

When I opened my eyes I wasn't in the graveyard, but I was still looking down on a bleeding hand, only the hand did not belong to me. Grasped in the opposite hand was a long slender dagger with an intricate handle. I was speaking into a small fire in front of me, but in a new language. I was able to translate it, just as I did in my regression as Brandt:

"Blood seals the curse of the soul. Fire turns the blood to ash. With this sacrifice I ask the Gods to change their fates. Let unrested souls fly free from mine."

Tiny fireworks ignite in the flames as his blood meets the embers. I watch with amazement as each drop sparks. He takes the knife and draws a symbol in the sand at his feet and kneels, repeating the prayer. I've seen this image before. It's astrological, but I can't place it. The image is starting to wave, like film caught in a projector. My thoughts feel dizzy, but his are steady. I try to fight it, to place where I am, who I am, but I'm blocked from it. I can only watch what is in front of me through his eyes.

I turn to find a woman lying on a raised pedestal behind me. She is still, yet the rosy color in her cheeks reflects the fire's glow. I kneel beside her, resting my head on her arm. His prayer appears in my head, in English. He whispers under his breath beside her.

"The blood of my blood protects her. May the God's let her spirit free to run to the next life. Free of burden. Free of hardship. Free of me. Though her life be short, it rings eternal. With this sacrifice, I save her."

He whispers these words over and over again until the graze of a hand interrupts him. He lifts his head slowly to meet her gaze. Her brown eyes are set ablaze with flecks of gold. Clusters of gold freckles stare back at me. Her eyes are like a kaleidoscope. A smile graces her lips. I feel a tear trickle down my face.

"I'm going to save you, my love. I will find you again. I promise." She looked at him with a furrowed brow. In that moment, I know it's Liv. In that moment, I know what I am about to do.

My mind is screaming, but his thoughts are steady. I rise, bringing her face to mine in a kiss. Just as we depart, as her eyes find mine, my dagger meets her chest. Her eyes fill with confusion and pain. She is struggling to speak, but I silence her with my hand, her eyes borrowing into mine. Finally, the flecks disperse and she is gone.

Her blood is spilling onto my free hand. It's warm and sticky between my fingers. I can't breath. The image is starting to fade away. I hear sirens in the distant present. I fall into the black.

My eyes open to Liv's blue eyes staring at me with that same confused look. The light of the sirens catch a glimmer in her eye. A small fleck of gold peeks out amongst a sea of blue. The common thread amongst all my lives lies within that freckle. There is still more to discover about our pasts, but I'm not sure if I want to uncover it.